The
TRUTH
in the
LIE

Arthur Klepfisz

Evil can be contagious,

readily caught and taught,

difficult to get rid of.

First published by Busybird Publishing 2023

ISBN
Print: 978-1-922954-59-6
Ebook: 978-1-922954-60-2

Cover design: Oscar Freeman/Busybird Publishing

Layout and typesetting: Busybird Publishing

Busybird Publishing
2/118 Para Road
Montmorency, Victoria
Australia 3094
www.busybird.com.au

About the Author

Arthur Klepfisz was born in Poland in 1941. When he was just a few months old, his parents were arrested and they were all placed in a labour camp where they remained for nine months until a policeman helped them escape. A month later, the camp and its inhabitants were destroyed. Most of Arthur's family perished during the Holocaust. 

Arthur studied medicine and trained to be a psychiatrist. He experienced three years of orchestrated attacks by Scientology through the media. They used accusations of deep-sleep therapy to underminine the public's trust in psychiatric care. It finally ended in a court battle where Judge Wendy Wilmoth ruled in Arthur's favour, describing his management of patients as exemplary, and found the evidence of hostile witnesses lacking in credibility.

After the court case Arthur sued a media outlet successfully.

In many ways, *The Truth in the Lie* can be seen as a fictional biography as it details events that Arthur experienced to some degree.

Though English was Arthur's second language he got 100% for English in high school and it was suggested he become a writer professionally. However, his medical career left little time for this.

Exceptions were undertaking a writing course with author Andrea Goldsmith and obtaining a distinction, writing the book *An Eye For An Eye*, and coming 8th in a short story competition in Atlanta, USA.

Chapter 1

It was a balmy day in Riverdale, upstate New York, in the late 1960s; the end of a crazy decade.

It began with Freedom Riders bussing into the American South, challenging segregation, and a Russian cosmonaut, Yuri Gagarin, becoming the first human to fly into space. East Germany began construction of the Berlin Wall, President Kennedy okayed the disastrous Bay of Pigs invasion, and there was a build-up of the US military presence in Vietnam.

It was a time of flux and varying perceptions. America was moving out of the post–World War 2 era, but there was no guarantee of worldwide security or peace. In place of overt war, a Cold War was beginning to develop. The Soviet Union and the United States moved from being allies against Nazi Germany to jostling for superiority in this post-war period.

As the Soviet Union tightened its grip on Eastern Europe, the United States was active in preventing the spread of communist influence in Western European nations such as France, Italy and Greece. The perception of who was friend and who was foe had become complex once more.

At the same time, in the town of Riverdale, the ground was covered with a mosaic of speckled leaves, blood red and butter yellow. And in a seedy motel room, which one could rent by the hour, two figures lay together, acting out their differing needs.

Brian Wright groaned, glanced at the clock on the wall, then roughly pushed down on the soft figure clinging to him. He looked at the clock again and thrust harder and faster, eliciting squeals of pain. Silently he repeated the mantra that had ruled his life as far back as he could recall: Thou shall not feel sorry for thyself but rather get even. Or, as his comic strip heroes declared, 'Don't get hurt. Get even.'

Not far away, the woman's husband lay on his own, gasping his last breath.

Once more Brian checked the time, then rolled off the sobbing figure beneath him and exited the room, his face carrying a hint of a smile.

Chapter 2

Jerome awoke and wished he hadn't. The clock on the wall revealed that it was 6:10 am, removing any justification for rolling over and going back to sleep. As he looked around, he realised he was the only one in the ward who seemed fully awake. He grimaced – being awake carried no real benefits.

He recalled the daily ritual he'd put himself through in the past, trying to ensure he got up on time throughout his working life. The mornings used to be hellish for him, as inevitably he struggled to wake up on time and felt dazed when he did so. Eventually, in desperation, he devised a ritual that used three alarm clocks, two placed close by his bed and the third partially hidden some distance away. It wasn't truly hidden as he knew its location; it just wasn't nearby. To turn off this third clock, he had to stagger to a chest of drawers and extract the timepiece from under a pile of socks in the second drawer. Day after day, year after year, he'd clung to this ritual, which would have sounded bizarre to others but worked for him. Without it, he was at risk of waking up in the afternoon.

Eventually, sleep specialists told him he had a sleep disorder. It was fine giving it a label, but he felt none of the treatments they gave him helped in any significant way. With the ritual of the three clocks, however, he'd begin moving slowly as the first two went off, and by the time he shut down the third he was able to have breakfast and then arrive at his 8 am lecture or ward round at 7:30 am, reasonably alert.

Now, in his ward at Riverdale Psychiatric Hospital, the noise emanating from staff and from other patients waking up was beginning to achieve a similar result in getting him moving in the morning. It was, however, a less pleasant sequence than the three alarm clocks.

Jerome became aware of the fluorescent lights above him, noting the bluish glare they cast, which coated the varicosed cracked-plaster walls. A heavy atmosphere and the pungent odour of disinfectant hung low in the room. There appeared to be no feasible way that sunlight, or life itself, could penetrate here.

Jerome's psychiatric ward was on the ground floor of the hospital and was all-male, with space for 14 men suffering severe psychiatric disorders and admitted on an involuntary basis. This meant they did not have the freedom to discharge themselves whenever they wished, as discharge was dependent on the treating doctor deciding they were well enough to warrant release from the hospital.

As Jerome looked around, he could see increasing movement as patients were roused by the lights and the comings and goings of staff. Although he'd only been admitted to the ward 24 hours before, he was already troubled by the sight of patients struggling to wake and get out of bed. He was particularly bothered by the lack of visible interaction between them, and how they uniformly appeared to be mute and had milky eyes, suggesting the blinds had been drawn on life. He wondered whether they themselves chose to lower the blinds or whether others had done it for them. Their movements were uncoordinated and fragmented, like the wooden dolls in a pantomime Jerome had seen when he was very young.

From what Jerome had been told, the patients in his ward had been diagnosed as either psychotic or borderline psychotic. His assessment was that they looked like zombies, dead before their time. It seemed bizarre to Jerome that someone like him, who wanted to train as a consultant psychiatrist, would now find himself on the receiving end of psychiatric care of this nature.

Although uncomfortable with what he was witnessing, Jerome found he couldn't take his eyes off the figures around him. He was mesmerised by their foggy eyes and the occasional sound and stench of agony. Their movements were often repetitive and, to an outside observer like himself, lacking in purpose. Some of them showed an obsessive, detached preoccupation with minutiae, and they all appeared devoid of interest in the people around them. It was as if they were each living alone on an island, with their surroundings not registering in their consciousness.

There were three other wards in this private teaching psychiatric hospital, each administering to less severely disturbed patients. There, patients had the freedom of deciding for themselves when they were ready to be discharged, though it was recommended they consult their treating doctor about their conclusions. If a doctor and a patient happened to disagree on the date of discharge, the patients had the freedom to follow their own decision. This was in marked contrast to the patients in the closed ward where Jerome was now housed, and in his ward, patients were only discharged if their doctor recommended that course of action.

Jerome had difficulty imagining himself as a therapist interacting with the other men in his ward, and he reminded himself that he would have to learn how to do that when his training in psychiatry formally began. He could see how difficult it would be when everyone around him, including the staff, appeared to show little interest in anyone else, but rather were consistently oblivious of each other.

When Jerome was admitted, he'd been impressed by the parkland-type grounds surrounding the hospital. There were several acres of wooded land, with a small stream twisting its way through the area. It felt very serene, but there was a jarring contrast between the natural environment and the large slab of a building that was the psychiatric hospital itself. It presented as a mass of bricks with small windows guarded by rusting metal bars, with the entire structure walled off from the serenity of the parklands by a high-wire enclosure. The sight of these security measures troubled Jerome, who felt it was more suited to a custodial prison than a psychiatric hospital.

Inside, the heavy, drab furnishings did nothing to soften the exterior image, nor did they diminish the discomfort Jerome experienced. The fluorescent lights cast harsh shadows throughout the stark interior, including what seemed like bottomless pits under

In chronic borderline psychotic ward with illness and
excessive sedation removing this patient from life.

the patient's metal-frame beds, which were arrayed close to each other. Each bed had a plastic curtain that could be drawn around it, the plastic a mottled yellow that looked like urine stains.

Jerome's fellow patients did not appear to feel the lack of cheer as he did. A combination of illness and sedation left them devoid of any expressive emotion, including envy – they were not aware of missing out. It was as if they were busy blocking out most of the world around them. At night, however, the various terrors tormenting them came alive and took hold, and their fears became palpable. Riverdale itself seemed a middle-class town from the brief look Jerome had on his arrival. He'd read that it housed a population of about 20,000 people, many of whom worked in jobs they owed to a wealthy industrialist whose factories produced bicycles, as well as tyres for bikes and cars. It did not appear to be a town whose residents found it exciting, as on the weekend large numbers would exit the place, presumably headed for the bright lights and fleshpots of more lively locales such as New York.

What wasn't yet apparent to Jerome was the somewhat dark underside of Riverdale. It was too early for him to see that Riverdale was a colour-coded township rife with conflict and tension between its black and white residents. He had yet to hear about the sporadic race riots to which police reacted in an overly aggressive way, nor had he heard how crimes were often ascribed to black folk even when there was no strong proof. But he had already noted that in the hospital, the more menial jobs were carried out by dark-skinned people. He'd also realised that in his own ward there were no black nurses. Jerome had encountered Carlos, a black nursing aide who appeared friendly in the brief contact they'd had, or at least a lot friendlier than any of the other nursing staff, but even this appeared to be an elevation beyond what most other black people could aspire to.

It troubled Jerome to see people judged by their colour, especially as he was aware that several countries over the years believed that people with intellectual and psychiatric deficits, as well as people who weren't white, should be eliminated to avoid 'contamination' of the general population. Jerome's family had direct experience of how being Jewish could equate to a death sentence. Such purification attitudes had been more openly put forward around the 1940s, but two decades later they still had their adherents, and when these people perceived a receptive audience, they would hold forth on these warped views.

As Jerome considered what he'd learnt about the township of Riverdale, and the developing impression of the psychiatric hospital now housing him, he began to feel a cold sliver of doubt sliding through his body. He felt he was beginning to understand why so many townspeople left the city at the weekend. He felt irritated that the sources he'd relied on to help him decide which was the best American psychiatric program to apply for, had failed to mention these factors, and he wondered how much they would interfere with his day-to-day life later. He wasn't sure whether he was to blame for what in hindsight appeared to be inadequate research, or whether the sources he drew on failed to give accurate in-depth information. On balance, he blamed the sources. He had put in six weeks of what he considered was intensive research, which he continued to believe should have been sufficient, and Riverdale had come up smelling sweet.

Jerome turned his attention to the man who lay in the bed alongside his, whom he considered unlike the other patients. When Jerome had been admitted, this man had taken the initiative and introduced himself as Tom. Tom was middle-aged, and if one was asked to describe him, the word that would come to mind was 'plump'. He was round all over, with a pot belly and cheeks as ruddy as marzipan fruit. Even his laughter sounded plump. Jerome, by contrast, was wiry and strong. Whilst Tom had approached him open-eyed, Jerome had eyes that were only vigilant and alert when other eyes weren't meeting his. When they did, they'd find him gazing into the distance, avoiding any shared experience.

Last night, Jerome had been woken by the pain of Tom's screaming nightmare. However, even this sign of obvious distress had not altered Jerome's feeling that somehow, he and Tom might have something in common, that they both differed from the others in the ward. Jerome had gone on to wonder whether Tom was strong enough to be treated on an outpatient basis, before reminding himself that it was presumptuous of him to jump to that conclusion, especially as Tom had already confided that he'd been an inpatient in Riverdale for close to two years.

The card on Jerome's bed showed him to be one Jerome Silver and listed his treating psychiatrists as Dr. Ludwick Klein and Dr. Stephen Anderson. Of course, both his name and the file notes associated with his admission were fictitious, the brainchildren of the two doctors Klein and Anderson who headed the psychiatric units. Hidden by this-persona of Jerome Silver was Brian Wright of Birmingham UK, the man who had graduated as a young medical doctor in England, then applied to study psychiatry at Riverdale.

He felt he had been roped into an experiment and would resume his former life when he was 'discharged' after several weeks, ready to commence his academic psychiatric training. He continued to berate himself at having been so impulsive. He had chosen Riverdale to provide his psychiatric training course, and whilst it had its positives, he was gradually becoming aware of potential deficits in the environment of the hospital and the town it was housed in.

Certainly, there would be a broad spectrum of ideas that he might be exposed to, with lectures and supervision from a range of psychiatrists. There were the four psychiatrists with permanent positions at the hospital – Klein, Anderson, Lynch and Roberts – and a number of others who had private practices in the area and also did sessional work at the hospital. Added to this input would be lectures from eminent psychiatrists touring through the area.

Jerome hadn't had an opportunity to look at the layout of the hospital, but the paperwork and photographs had revealed that there were two impressive lecture halls and three other wards in addition to the involuntary ground-floor one where he was an inpatient. The other wards could house about 15 patients each, on a voluntary basis. There seemed to be little need for psychiatric assistance in the ground-floor psychosis ward. Sister Rote exerted total control over patient management in that ward, with the occasional doctor called in to review the medication. The approach tended to accept that the patients in the ground-floor ward didn't communicate verbally, so there was little point in trying to speak to them, with a reliance on medication alone. When a new patient was first admitted, in theory they would come with a letter of referral expressing concern about the patient's condition. This letter may have been written by a doctor in private practice working outside the hospital, or it may have been a doctor associated with the hospital who saw the patient in an outpatient clinic. Gradually, the medical students training in psychiatry provided additional therapeutic assistance to the other wards.

Doctors Klein and Anderson had set up a research project whereby a healthy individual would be hospitalised in Riverdale Hospital's locked ward. This patient was to be unknown to the staff and to the local community. The two doctors felt Brian would be an ideal candidate for their trial as he would have only recently arrived from another country and would be totally anonymous to the town's residents. And so, after Brian had accepted the task, (did he have any other option?), they'd created a fictitious history for a Jerome Silver. They'd also explained to hospital staff that because Jerome was so ill and held such a high level of suspicion, it was imperative that only Klein or Anderson prepare and administer his medication.

Only the three conspirators would then know it was a placebo that was being administered to their patient.

The main focus of the project was to assess whether the treating staff of doctors and nurses in Jerome's ward would independently evaluate this new patient's condition and diagnosis, or whether they would merely echo what was already written in his letter of referral (which in Jerome's case contained fabricated judgements created by Klein and Anderson). In other words, he was essentially a healthy man, without any identifiable psychiatric disorder, whose presentation and history had been dressed up to create the image of a man with major psychiatric problems.

Klein and Anderson were posing the question as to whether the acquired label they had created would stick to Jerome, and become a permanent fixture, rather than future doctors treating Jerome forming their own independent assessment.

The professional understanding applied to all patients newly admitted to the ward was that the doctors and other staff on duty at the time, would do their own independent assessment and formulate their own diagnosis. However, Klein and Anderson had long suspected that most staff took the easy route, perpetuating the diagnosis previously arrived at by those who'd had past contact with the patient. In other words, once a patient was labelled, that label might be glued to them for life.

There were also side issues that the psychiatrists were interested in exploring to some degree, keeping in mind the relatively short period of time available to them with this pretend patient. They wanted to observe how a healthy patient might interact with and impact the other patients in the ward who suffered from genuine psychiatric illnesses. Was it possible that the presence of a healthy person could in some way stimulate some of the chronic patients, so that they came to life in varying degrees and commenced interacting with those around them?

In addition, Klein and Anderson wondered if, in the future, assuming this initial trial went well, other trainee psychiatrists could be admitted as inpatients in the hope the experience would assist them in developing a deeper level of empathy towards the patients they were treating. They postulated it might help treating staff understand the sense of powerlessness and loss of independence that so many of the chronic patients in the ward experienced. They were aware that the limited time available to them would at best give them a clearer idea as to how they would set up future trials.

Despite these worthy aims, Jerome had felt somewhat anxious about being thrust into this situation of playing the role of a man with a severe psychiatric disorder and being put yet again into a position of falsehood and lying. Yet he'd felt he couldn't say no and kept these concerns to himself. "After all," he said to himself, given that he was the person he conversed with the most, "if I pursue my studies at Riverdale, the men who would give me the thumbs up, telling me I passed, or the opposite would be Klein and Anderson."

He realised somewhat bitterly their offer of taking part in their trial was really no offer. It was a demand; do it or fail your psychiatric training. He hoped to earn some gold points by pleasing the two psychiatrists with his compliance.

However, the major cause of Jerome's discomfort when he'd been asked to take part in the secret research was related to his passionately held wish of wanting to stop living a lie. He desperately craved to have people see him for the person he was and have them learn to like that person – the real Brian. Somewhat bitterly, Jerome reflected on how, for most of his life, the way he was perceived was constantly altered if not controlled by others, mostly to his disadvantage. The view others had of him too often was coloured by negative factors detached and separate from himself.

Having come from a severely dysfunctional family, Jerome had long suffered the soul-destroying feeling that, no matter how well he did or whatever he achieved, it was always diminished in the eyes of the people around him. They only saw him as the son of those two 'alcoholic bums', never as a desirable person in his own right, and it was for this reason his peers wanted nothing to do with him socially.

Thus, after he graduated in Medicine in Birmingham, he'd applied to several overseas institutions whose psychiatric training programs boasted good reputations, finally settling on the program offered in Riverdale. In the United States, he would be anonymous. His family would be invisible, and people could relate to him as the person they perceived in front of them, not as the offspring of an undesirable couple. For Jerome, this would be a godsend, as he desperately sought the opportunity to be himself in other people's eyes, with qualities he predicted they could and would admire. This research trial was just delaying the process a bit. He now wondered whether he had rushed his decision about suitable psychiatric training.

Jerome believed that for most of his life he'd had to pretend and at times lie, so he could hide some aspect of himself from the scrutiny of others. There was a time in his life when he hid being Jewish, a time when he hid who his parents were. Ironically, he was now hiding the fact that he was healthy and did not need treatment in this psychiatric ward. In this ward, once again no-one wanted anything to do with him, except Tom. Then again, the other patients didn't appear to have an interest in anyone else either.

Once admitted to the ward, Jerome had thought there was no possible way the staff here would continue to believe that he needed hospitalisation for psychiatric reasons. He imagined it wouldn't be long before someone on the floor, be it a member of staff or a patient, confronted him, demanding to know what sort of game he was playing.

Chapter 3

Lying in bed, Jerome felt as if he was in a cinema, watching a movie unfold. He mused that it was along the lines of an old Charlie Chaplin silent movie, as no-one in the ward spoke to anyone else. The thought popped into his mind that the Rolling Stones' song '*I Can't Get No Satisfaction*' could have been inspired by a place similar to where he was now housed. He knew he had better start moving himself as he couldn't merely be an observer forever.

Tom was already dressed when Jerome glanced in his direction again. With a grin, Tom said, 'Hi Jerome. Ready for the delicacies the chef has created this morning?'

Jerome smiled, having already decided how he would eat the minimum required to survive and to avoid drawing staff attention to himself. Two weeks or so of hospital food wouldn't be a treat, but he was sure he could handle it for that limited period of time.

As he began to rapidly dress, retrieving clothes from a locker beside his bed, Jerome reminded himself of the need to concentrate and make sure he responded to the name 'Jerome' when speaking to other people. It would be a bummer if someone called out 'Jerome!' and he looked around to see who they were talking to.

The idea of his true identity made him think back to when, as Brian Wright, he had phoned the Riverdale Psychiatric Hospital and applied to do his psychiatric training there, at the same time asking for suggestions about accommodation that he could arrange in the vicinity. He rang the very first number he was given, which turned out to be a quite appealing option. It was a boarding house very close to the hospital, renting rooms at what he felt was a reasonable cost. He discovered they wouldn't lock him into a lease, and if it proved unsuitable after he got there, he could terminate the arrangement without any significant penalty.

On arriving at the boarding house, Brian met Mrs Sykes, who ran the accommodation. She was a particularly large lady, with the overall appearance of a Dickensian character. She had a loud booming voice, was solid in stature, and enforced a definite set of rules that she expected all boarders to abide by. She asked that everyone call her Mrs Sykes, and it was apparent that she liked the place to run like clockwork, or as she put it, 'Everything should have a place and every place should have a name.' Although she appeared strict in most ways, Brian sensed that there was a fair degree of kindness underneath the bluster.

Brian chuckled to himself as he recalled Mrs Syke's statement that 'every place should have a name'. Given the research the two head psychiatrists had involved him in, he was requested by them to maintain the identity of Jerome Silver until he left the Riverdale program, a matter of weeks.

Two other people would be staying at the boarding house at the same time as himself, and although not having yet met them, Brian hoped they would be reasonably compatible. However, they were not likely to have all that much contact together given his expected long hours at work plus the following hours of study he had to do when he went to his accommodation after work.

Despite the anxiety and apprehension that he often experienced, Brian had also become aware of a sense of excitement at the coming opportunity to live in an environment where he dared hope to forge a new identity, where no one knew him nor would they judge him by his past. He was going to live in a new city, in a new country, learning a new specialty of medicine. He would be anonymous with a clean slate. He believed people would like the person they saw, without his family influencing their judgement.

He felt as if his whole life had been one of confronting hurdles, obstacles that he had to surmount to be able to function, to get somewhere in the race of life. He believed he had managed to do that, but at what cost? And anyway, how do you measure whether you've cleared a hurdle? You might get over one, but what if you find that doing so takes so much out of you that you're now running last? Are you any better off then? 'Probably yes,' he thought, 'as you're still competing.'

Brian and his family had survived the Holocaust, whilst living in Poland during World War II, where being Jewish was more about being a target than a religion. In other words, while death was part of the normal cycle of life, for Jews it became part of being Jewish. He had no real memories of that time but had learnt a lot from what he had been told, as well as records of what had occurred. The things that were 'missing' from his own history could often be intuited from knowledge of what had happened to so many other people in his position. It was rammed home even more by the absence of grandparents, uncles and aunts in his own life. He had never confided in anyone that he didn't realise the large gap that existed in his family structure before he and his parents came to live in England as refugees.

How can you realise you lost something when you can't recall ever having had it? He had no memory of a life surrounded by uncles, aunts, grandparents, cousins. He had no photos to remind him that there was a time when grandparents and other family members existed. It was only when he and his parents escaped to the UK that he witnessed the extended family glue that generated love and warmth within many families. He thought and thought and didn't feel comfortable asking his parents to help him make sense of it. The few photos his parents appeared to possess were of him and them with holes disfiguring the pictures. His parents were short with him when he asked about the holes but eventually with tight lips snapped that the holes had removed friend's faces to protect them. It was sometime later that they could bring themselves to name the Holocaust and persecution of Jews. It was another Jewish family who were friends of his parents who elaborated how his family and other families hid by adopting false identities during the Holocaust and how the holes protected others. Brian recalled asking, 'What do you mean?' hoping to fill the gaps as his parents were reluctant to discuss these experiences.

With lowered eyes and tight voice, a male friend of his parents explained. 'Those holes stop you identifying who your parent's friends were and could save their lives if the Nazis caught your parents.'

In Birmingham Brian discovered the holes in family photos where friends had been removed, and the holes in his family tree where branches of the family tree had been lopped off and killed.

In Birmingham, began his struggle of dealing with a loss he never knew he had, until he saw other families and became aware of what was missing in his own.

When playing in the park and seeing kids his age laughing, yelling gleefully and holding hands with these elderly midgets who gave the kids sweets and ice creams, it was then the hole in his family life started feeling real and raw.

As a young adult it troubled him that, even in the absence of a direct memory of events during the Holocaust, it continually had a major impact on his life. Simply put, he felt it was stuffing up his life, and he resented the time and emotion it extracted from him. He was absolutely sure it had damaged his parents physically and emotionally, creating the toxic environment in which he'd grown up. He felt there was a danger; it had removed love and created bitterness. There was no one he felt able to ask but the thought festered whether it was doing the same thing to him as it had to his parents. Missing was a key word for Brian. Not only were many memories missing, but what was also missing were the people who normally created the fabric and warmth of extended family life. There were no grandparents, no uncles or aunts, no memories of extended family. He believed that one needed to have knowledge of both the past and present to give adequate meaning to future life.

As Brian strove to make sense of the differences between his own family life and that of many others around him, he became increasingly aware that he had been robbed. His environment was barren of sights, a blank canvas, bereft of laughter and love. So many of his memories had been lost or stolen from him, and he feared they would be missing forever. As he heard the joyful laughter of family get togethers in Birmingham, he sensed the bitterness rising within him.

He felt his memory constantly zigzagging. There were recollections he'd rather forget and many more he wished he could retrieve. He found he had been left with only scraps of recall, creating a fear that this void would deprive his life of the nourishment required to make it thrive. He needed a past and a present if there was to be a sense of continuity and purpose as he looked to the future. The whole situation effectively left him floundering, struggling to find meaning in most of what he thought or did.

Even though he had few direct memories of the ravages of the Holocaust he felt it had damaged his parents physically and emotionally and created the toxic environment he grew up in.

Brian was very aware that feeling this way fragmented his nature, created an underlying anger and resentment that could flare up and trouble him with its severity. Somewhat bitterly he told himself, 'Physician, heal thyself.'

He found himself dreaming a lot, often feeling the worse for it. He began to question why he couldn't learn to control what dreams he had on any particular night, asking himself bitterly, 'It's my brain, so why can't it follow my orders?' He often yearned for a vision-dispensing machine, allowing him to select his dreams and be in control of them, rather than having the dreams controlling and overwhelming him. Not for the first time, there was a sizeable gap between what he wished for and what he believed feasible. Now he was in a psychiatric ward, he realised he was not alone as far as the terrors of the night were concerned.

Occasionally, he reflected on how dreadful it would be to be totally devoid of memories or positive feelings or hopes, akin to vegetating. He couldn't prevent the feeling, one that ate away at him, that a significant part of his life had been taken away and could never be retrieved. There was only a minor percentage of time left in which he could still construct a meaningful life, producing what most people, including himself, viewed as normal.

At first, Brian had wondered why people in Birmingham had focused on his parents and constantly run them down, and consequently devalued Brian himself. Of course, what poisoned their perception of his parents was not only that they drank to excess; this was not a unique problem in the area where they lived. What had clinched the bottom rung of the ladder for them was that his stepfather was a violent bully who had accumulated a string of assault charges over the years, often by picking on people far less able to defend themselves. Like his wife. Thus, he had stripped Brian's mother of her warm personality, leaving a punching-bag persona.

All of this had led to Brian's obsessive preoccupation with the photographs that had documented his life in a patchy fashion over the years. He believed that it was vital to hang on to the documented pieces of his life and attempt to connect them as best he could, to make sense of the bigger picture. Nevertheless, Brian's experience of life often took on the desperate quality of a drowning man hanging on by his fingertips to a floating plank of wood in a dark, vast ocean devoid of memories.

○

Jerome had the urge to photograph his ward at the hospital, including a photograph for posterity of Tom, who seemed to have become a special, totemic figure in Jerome's life in an amazingly short period of time. Tom, having made the decision that this ward was now his home, had equipped himself with more than the basics. When he heard Jerome's wish to take photos, he offered Jerome the use of his relatively new 35mm Canon camera. When the use of the camera was offered, Jerome repeated the promise that he only intended to photograph people in the ward if they and Tom were comfortable having him do it.

Jerome yearned to get permission from Tom to document the details of their own interaction, painfully aware of how difficult it was to put together the jigsaw of his own life. It was as if he feared the possible loss of yet another memory and did not want to add to the gaps in his knowledge of the past. He was determined to document his life in as clear a fashion as he could.

In contrast there were times he was aware of sidestepping reality. He had become painfully aware of avoiding mirrors whenever he could. He sensed the mirrors revealed the ravages of his past life, a litany of failures, and there was an absence of warmth and happiness in the images they showed him. He couldn't shake the feeling of not being a complete person, but rather a fragmented partial person, always carrying some hidden fact or secret to do with himself. He frequently asked himself how others could relate to someone like that, how they could ever get a meaningful grasp of him emotionally. At moments of painful honesty, he had to admit to himself that he was creating a self-fulfilling prophecy, that he prevented people getting close even if they were so inclined.

What bothered him most looking at his mirror image were the dilated pupils, and the furrowed brow with some moisture that he'd wipe off with a tissue. This was the harsh reality, without the scope that a photo provided to soften the image.

Jerome grimaced as he thought back to the words of his landlady Mrs Sykes, about everything having a place and every place having a name. Maybe he could yet make sense and purpose out of his chaos.

Jerome felt his thoughts were flying in all directions. A part of him was excited at the prospect of following his long-held dream of studying and learning the skills that would ultimately allow him to work as a psychiatrist. There was also the excitement about people seeing him as the person he was, not judging him by factors that weren't of his making, like his drunken parents. However, part of him warned that it was too early to rejoice, as things rarely worked out the way one hoped.

As living proof of that doubt, here he was, starting this new life in Riverdale with a lie, or rather with his professors asking him to live out a lie. Sure, it wouldn't be forever, but would his fellow patients forgive him for the lie?

He thought back to the first meeting he'd had with Dr. Klein and Anderson. The two men were very different, both physically and in personality. Klein was a small, compact man with a neat presentation, starting with his finely turned moustache and neat jacket and tie. It was a relief to detect that under this somewhat rigid exterior there appeared to be a degree of sensitivity and humour. He recalled how, after spelling out what 'Jerome' had to do in this trial of pretending to be a patient, Klein had looked him straight in the eye and in a stern voice said, 'And if you stuff this up I will put an old Jewish curse on you. You know the one, where you lose all your teeth except one, and you have a toothache in that one for the rest of your life.' Klein then burst out laughing.

Anderson, a tall, athletic-looking man who reportedly had been a good sportsman in his youth, hadn't said much during their meeting, which took place outside the hospital, so as not to have Jerome meet any other staff until he'd been admitted as a hospital patient. Mostly, Anderson gave the impression of following Klein's lead.

Both professors emphasised the need for secrecy, to not discuss the experiment with anyone else. They had documented what they were setting up in private notes filed at Klein's home away from prying eyes of other staff.,. They believed if anyone else was told, the risk of it being leaked during idle chatter would be high.

As Jerome grappled with this fusillade of thoughts and emotions, he became aware that Tom was patiently waiting for Jerome to join him in going to breakfast. Tom hadn't yet complained, but Jerome felt he had better pull his finger out.

Most of the ward was now stirring, and staff members were going around making sure that everyone was getting mobilised. They did not interact with the patients in a friendly manner, as far as Jerome could see, except for Carlos of course. The remainder of the staff seemed almost oblivious of the patients' existence, apart from issuing the occasional instruction or order. Their behaviour suggested a custodial role.

Jerome watched as Sister Rote walked by, with hardly a glance in his direction. Tom had told him that many patients referred to her as Rote the Rottweiler. She was probably just short of 5 feet tall, a diminutive figure, but when in full flight and angry, which Tom said was often, she could seem a lot bigger. She had large protruding middle teeth, and severe acne which had left her face pitted with craters. She kept her hair in a tight bun and altered the contours of her body by severely strapping her breasts so that they were hidden as much as possible.

Sister Rote oversaw the running of Jerome's ward. Tom had explained how people appeared to step aside and avoid crossing her path whenever possible. Even in the short time he had been there, Jerome felt that he could almost smell the fear generated whenever Sister Rote was close by. Some patients even hugged the walls as she bustled by. And Tom told him that the other staff – and by that he meant all of them – became snappier and abrasive when she was near.

When Tom had confided to Jerome that Sister Rote was an absolute bitch and a ball-cutter, Jerome had playfully teased him. He told Tom that Rote the Rottweiler was probably the Angel of Mercy in disguise, loving humanity all night long and wrung out by the time she reached the ward, with nothing left to give.

Sister Rote alone amongst the staff wore a white starched uniform, while the others were dressed in mufti, or street clothes. She was also the only female staff member on that floor. Tom had giggled quietly as he told Jerome that the way to pick which people were staff, given the absence of uniforms, was by noting if they had keys dangling from their waist. The staff members were the ones who could open locks in the ward.

Tom added that Carlos had explained the reason why the staff, besides Sister Rote, didn't have uniforms – it was to make them seem less threatening to the patients. Jerome felt that explanation wasn't logical, as the patients were already mentally confused, struggling to hold on to reality, and the lack of a differentiating uniform would only confuse them further.

Tom and Jerome walked together to breakfast, with a plan to sit side by side. Jerome didn't feel particularly hungry, but he knew it was important to present as a 'good patient'. And so, the pair were herded by staff down dim corridors and into the dining area. It turned out to be a long, narrow, soulless room, as poorly lit as the corridors. In the centre of the room was a long table sandwiched between two rough-looking wooden benches, where the fourteen patients sat next to each other. There was an absence of decoration or warmth.

In a way, the poor lighting suited Jerome, as it created a veil behind which he could sit unnoticed and observe. He did not feel comfortable being there. In fact, the experience simply added to his discomfort at not yet having been seen by the two psychiatrists who had set up the project, as had been agreed at their first meeting.

At that meeting they explained how they would 'assess' him in the first day or two of his stay. He told himself they had merely been held up and would come in the evening, yet he wasn't sure he totally believed himself.

When Jerome remarked on how primitive the dining area room's furnishings were, particularly the benches, Tom agreed that it felt like they were sitting on splinters. With a straight face, Jerome then asked, 'Do you know who has the contract for interior decorating in this place?'

Tom, with a slight smile gracing his face, said, 'Can't help you with that Jerome, but you could put in a quote if you're interested.'

Allowing himself a broader grin, Jerome chuckled and said, 'Well, if there's a special on grey paint, I reckon I could be really competitive. Of course, I could offer a change of colour, like black, but I doubt that would be preferred.'

When some staff members walked by, with their eyes looking only straight ahead, Jerome said 'G'day' and grinned at them, but the response matched the colour of the room.

'Do they ever speak to you, Tom?' Jerome queried. 'If I had to guess, it's probably only when they're telling you what to do or what not to do.'

Tom continued to smile. 'Yeah, I suppose in a way Carlos is the only one who interacts with me as if I existed. Actually, that's not accurate, because the matron does interact with me, although I wish she didn't. There's something about me that seems to irritate her. Must be my good looks.' He chuckled and theatrically smoothed his hair back.

'What do you think they feel about the patients?' Jerome asked, on impulse.

Tom thought for a moment and said, 'Like I told you before, Carlos treats me like I'm a real person, but I'm not totally sure what he feels about me or the other patients. And Rote only acknowledges me because I annoy the shit out of her.' He paused reflectively. 'I don't know what it is, really. Maybe because I don't seem scared of her, because I'm not. I heard from Dr. Klein that she feels I'm really sick and should be given a course of shock treatment. Luckily Klein was professional enough and bright enough to tell her, 'Not for the moment.' But you know what Jerome? For me, it's still easier living here than on the outside. I'll tell you more about that later.'

Jerome reflected that whilst it might suit Tom to discuss it in this way, it was not necessarily providing a tool that could help Jerome deal with his own emotional turmoil.

Tom seemed to pick up on this. 'I know it feels busy Jerome,' he said quietly, but try and be patient.

Tom and Jerome got up and joined the other patients who had queued to collect their breakfast. Two black men appeared to be responsible for dishing out the food, which they scooped onto plates from two large metallic containers on a trolley. The delicacies, as Tom had referred to them, looked to be a grey mash of cereal, half a boiled egg and a glass of milk. An optional red apple was available, which one could imagine housed a resident worm. Putting on weight would not be a risk here, Jerome thought to himself. There was also a single red capsule of medication per patient, which had to be swallowed immediately in front of a staff member, to ensure the patient consumed it.

Breakfast lasted just over an hour. The rest of the morning was spent creatively making stuffed toys and doing hand painting. The time dragged, but at lunch, Jerome and Tom sat together again in the dining hall.

Jerome had already told Tom about how he'd lived in Birmingham for a large part of his life and studied Medicine at one of the universities there. Now he confided to Tom that he had been shocked by some descriptions he had heard of the violence that had occurred in psychiatric hospitals in the United States. He repeated something Mrs Sykes had told him, about an episode several months earlier when the police in one city had brought an extremely disturbed man into a psychiatric institution to be committed. Unfortunately, the policeman escorting the person had not properly secured his gun holster. The man he was bringing in for treatment suddenly pulled the policeman's gun out of the holster and shot himself in the head, dying instantly. Jerome said that access to weapons was not something he'd been familiar with in England. He couldn't help but think that the man who pulled the gun out could just as readily have shot the policeman or one of the doctors or nurses. Either way, it was tragic.

Jerome explained that in England things appeared to be less violent in the hospital setting, that there could often be light-hearted banter between staff and those admitted, without anyone being put down. He smiled to himself as he recalled one particular patient, Pete, whom he had run into quite a few times in Birmingham. This man had chronic alcohol problems and regular admissions without evidence of any marked improvement. The thing about this man was that he was known to have a tattoo on his penis which could only be read clearly when the penis was erect. What was evident in that circumstance was 'I love Alice', with love represented by a picture of a heart. Apparently, Alice had been a lady the man had been in a long-term relationship with until they'd broken up several years back.

Even though the hospital was run by the Catholic Church, with nuns working as sisters in the wards, they appeared to tolerate a regular procession of medical students who came to examine Pete. The nuns had to be aware of what was going on, but they turned a blind eye to it, and it certainly made Pete cheerful. It seemed the case that during an examination of Pete's chest and abdomen, there was sufficient stimulation for a reading to be possible.

Jerome fell silent for a while, having told Tom quite a lot about himself, revealing the Brian part of him. As at breakfast, he wasn't hungry, but he felt that he better pretend to be and went through the motions by shuffling his food around on the plate and taking the occasional bite.

He felt increasingly troubled by not having seen Klein or Anderson since they had set up the project and brought him into this ward. It struck him that, in a way, he had gone from the dirt of the past to the prison of the present, and if the staff threw away the keys, he would be like a prisoner. He shrugged off this thought, realising that it was a nightmare scenario, not a real-life situation, though the moisture on his skin suggested he was far from convinced of this.

When he had met with Mrs Sykes, he'd told her he'd be away for a while, approximately three weeks, something to do with his studies. But he had also advised her not to get concerned if it was some days or a week longer than that before he returned. If that eventuated, he'd ring her, he promised. He now wondered how long he might be stuck in the ward, and if in fact a phone call would be necessary.

Jerome glanced down the table and noticed someone who had been pointed out to him at breakfast by Tom – a thin man with sunken features called Roger. Jerome had asked Tom to help him with the names of some of the other people in the room, and Roger was the first name he'd learned. However, this would likely prove not much of an advantage, as no-one apart from Tom amongst the patients seemed inclined to talk.

Lunch was dished out by the same two black kitchen aides he had seen at breakfast. The aides also appeared to have adopted the mute philosophy - why waste words when you can point. The menu was not extensive, consisting of hot soup (of uncertain origin), large, thick slices of bread put to rest in a toaster, several dollops of peanut butter, and doughnuts. Jerome watched Roger repeatedly go through the same routine as he devoured a doughnut, almost as if it would be his last meal, except for the fact that it was followed by another doughnut.

Jerome realised that he was tending to view the other patients as, in a way, dead before their time. To him they were just diagnoses, and this type of reaction troubled him. He knew that all human beings could suffer in various ways and that it was important to remember they were human beings. It would take a big effort, but he needed to stop judging the patients and allow sufficient time for trust to build up so that he and they could talk in depth. In other words, he had to talk to them and understand them as best he could, and gradually get to know the damaged people underneath. Whether any of this could occur in the short period of time he'd be a 'patient' remained to be seen.

Making this goal more difficult was the ongoing reaction he became aware of where he continued to be shocked by the fogged, milky, half-closed eyes of most of the men around him, and had checked in the mirror to reassure himself that his eyes differed. In addition, the pungent odour of disinfectant irritated his eyes and nostrils, and the lack of sunlight and conversation seemed to create a heavy weight that suppressed everything in the room.

It struck Jerome that even he was acting like a puppet, going through the motions, smiling from time to time, grimacing and frowning on demand at other times, as a counter to the static emotions around him.

To distract himself from these thoughts, Jerome suddenly asked Tom whether he had any thoughts on being discharged, and why it was that he had been there so long. Tom hesitated, and then, with a faint smile, said, 'Later, when we can sit down on our own, I'll tell you about it, and maybe you can tell me a bit about yourself as well.'

Jerome thanked him, and said he was looking forward to that, but wondered silently if he was pushing Tom a bit fast. He hesitated, then forged ahead, admitting to Tom that it surprised him how openly the two of them were able to talk to each other, and how quickly it had come about. He hesitated again before adding: 'Let me give you just one example of how the norm is that it takes people a long time to want to get to know me, or to feel they do know me.'

Tom nodded at this, which Jerome took as a green light for him to continue.

'I think I told you yesterday that I did very well academically in my final year at university…' Jerome took a deep breath, averted his gaze from Tom and in a soft but audible voice continued. 'When we had the presentation of awards, I was called up on stage and pronounced the top student for the year. Well, having the opportunity to say a few words, I decided right then that I would set some of the record straight. For pretty much the entire course I had been kept on the outer by the other students, and a large part of that had to do with what they thought of my family, which I'll tell you more about later. The teachers avoided intervening in any way and provided no support.

'So, there I am on the stage, and I began with, "I'm not going to say much," which provoked snickers around the room and some sarcastic cheers. I ignored them and said, "I want to teach you guys about context. Let me show you some numbers, you can write them down. Three, nine, thirteen, eighteen, twenty-eight, forty-one, forty-four. So, what do those numbers mean to you? Do you have any feelings about those numbers? If I had to guess, I'd say that they mean nothing to you. What if I now tell you that those were the winning numbers of the last British lottery, and the winner pocketed sixty-five million pounds? So how do you feel about those numbers now? Do they still mean nothing to you?" He let his question hang there for a while and locked eyes with Jerome, as if sharing his victory.

'I paused for a few seconds and then said, "We judge lots of things from the context they exist in. Most, or all of you, I think, have judged me over the years by my parents. You looked down on them and therefore looked down on me. You never took the trouble to see me as a person in my own rights. You knew nothing about why my parents were the way you saw them, nor were you interested in finding out. You labelled my parents alcoholic bums without understanding why they were like that. You then labelled me as a no-hoper, the son of those bums. You could never see me as an individual and relate to me as me."

'I left it at that and walked to my seat, determined not to run, probably with a faint smile on my face. There were a few claps, but largely silence, a considerable amount of it stunned. I made myself look around a bit and I knew that I had hit the target, given the stunned silence and the discomfort. But I had no illusions about it. I believed that a significant number of the people there would reject the message I'd tried to give. They would discard it and go on thinking the same way as before. A few of the staff who had taught us looked uncomfortable, but they kept quiet, pretending nothing had happened and avoiding my gaze.'

Tom stared intently at Jerome, then said, 'I'm impressed. That would have taken a lot of courage, Jerome.'

Chapter 4

DAY TWO

Jerome had now finished eating, but Roger was still devouring doughnuts. Jerome wasn't sure how many he'd eaten as he had not been keeping count. What he had noticed was a faint rail track that formed a grid on Roger's wrists, making him wonder if those marks were related to past episodes of self-harm. He was amazed at how much concentration Roger and quite a few of the others were applying to their food, smiling as he thought of the cliché, *You are what you eat.*

He then noticed Ewan, whose bed was close to his as well. Unlike the speed that Roger was showing in devouring his doughnuts, Ewan was slowly and carefully tracing the boundary of a pretzel with his tongue.

Jerome saw that Tom was watching him as he looked around, and they both smiled at each other. He was yet again struck by how amazing it was that he and Tom had developed such a bond in a short period of time, as this was not the norm for Jerome. Over the years he had developed a safety mechanism, the habit of waiting for people to make the first move, to reduce the danger of rejection. Telling Tom how close their relationship felt was way out of character for him. Normally, or rather abnormally, it would have made him feel vulnerable. Admitting someone is important to you is acknowledging that you'd be hurt if they withdrew that friendship. Somehow, he felt more confident with Tom, but not to the extent of letting him know that he possessed the potential for hurting Jerome.

Jerome now noticed another man, very short in stature and with folds and ridges of skin on all exposed areas. Jerome could not recall his name and asked Tom who it was. Tom replied that the man was named Swan and that he had set himself the task of continually reducing the number of chews per meal. Swan apparently had a deep-seated belief that it was a lot better for his health to chew less. Tom grinned as he explained that Swan had decided to go about it scientifically, not by eating less but by choosing foods that were soft, so that as he chewed, he could also gulp. Jerome could see that with the very soft foods, Swan was almost drinking them, with little chewing required.

Tom then nudged Jerome and said he had just remembered that the man's name was not Swan but in fact was Billy. It felt good to Jerome that Tom would go to the trouble of being accurate; and filling him in.

Jerome was impressed at how Tom knew the names of other patients as well as some of their history, suggesting there must have been some interaction to acquire these facts. He then reminded himself that Tom had graced these hallowed spaces for at least two years.

Once lunch was over, Jerome and Tom decided to stroll away and miss the occupational therapy class that had been organised, where they would make plaster moulds and do finger-painting.

They anticipated there might be some criticism and growling about it later, but not to the extent that it worried Tom, and he in turn reassured Jerome that it would be okay.

They exited the building and walked quite a way, to the more peripheral part of the hospital's grounds that was the designated area for the chronic patients. Jerome was somewhat surprised at how rapidly Tom walked without undue effort – he was obviously a lot fitter physically than his rounded appearance suggested. They chose a spot where it was unlikely they would bump into other people, lowering themselves onto a battered wooden seat overlooking a strip of greenery. A thin slice of river sat beyond that.

The patients in the ground-floor ward where Jerome and Tom were housed were not encouraged by staff to wander in the grounds, but they weren't prohibited from doing so. The fact was that the majority of these patients had no interest in wandering outside the ward, as they were caught up and imprisoned by their inner world and longings and had no interest nor courage in seeking a world beyond. Any inclination to possibly do so was further suppressed by the sedation from their medication. The few that did roam were well contained within the relatively small area bounded by high-wire fences.

When Jerome referred to what they were sitting on as a bench, Tom chuckled and again said it was more like a big splinter. They decided to christen it 'The Seat of Creation'.

They were silent for a short while, then Jerome tentatively turned towards his friend: 'Tom, look, I really don't want to be intrusive, but is it okay if I ask you something personal? Whether or not you want to answer is totally up to you.'

Tom gave a faint smile but said nothing. Jerome hesitantly went on: 'I really believe that you and I are somehow different to all the others in the ward. I don't think either one of us needs to be hospitalised in a ward like this. But you know what, Tom? More than anything else, I just can't understand why you've been in this hospital for close to two years and seem so accepting of it.' Jerome was now quite worried that he was being too intrusive, and this showed in his voice as he stuttered on: 'I have a feeling that you'd prefer to stay here rather than be discharged.'

Tom's blue eyes twinkled as he looked at Jerome. 'You're spot-on Jerome.' He leaned back and his eyes closed as he began recounting his story in a soft voice.

'My parents had a shit marriage, and they broke up when I was about eight years of age. As a single parent it was a real struggle for my mother; she had very little money or family support. She got cleaning jobs from time to time and somehow, we scraped by. Occasionally, other men came into her life and slept overnight, which made me uncomfortable. Eventually, the local priest persuaded my mum to put me into a Catholic boarding school. I'm not sure how much that cost her, but I think the Church helped to cover a lot of the cost. Anyway, the boarding school was hell for me. Some of the priests there were interested in me sexually. There was no-one I could turn to for help, and it went on for years. I tried to complain a couple of times to some of the priests who hadn't bothered me, but they weren't interested and did nothing. I only saw my mum occasionally and I felt it would be useless trying to tell her as she already wasn't coping and couldn't keep her own head above water. It caused permanent damage.'

Tom's voice was tight and barely audible, but he seemed determined to go on with his story.

'I'm sure it stopped me having normal relationships as I got older. I suffered bouts of depression and felt ashamed when I thought about it. It made me leave the Church and I became a loner.'

Jerome thought to himself that, despite this horrendous experience, underneath the wreckage Tom still had a great capacity for warmth and caring for others – although it was masked at times, possibly by the scars of his experiences.

Tom hesitated and was silent for a moment, then took a deep breath. And in a barely audible voice, 'You'll be surprised to hear that even though I was a loner, good fortune looked down on me and I met a gorgeous lady by the name of Sue, and we got married two months later. She was a motherly type and probably saw in me someone she could practise her mothering skills on. But fate was not going to let me get off so easily. Would you believe it - my brother Richard, who was two years younger than me, married my wife's sister, Jenny. He met her when she came to visit Sue. My brother and I were never alike and viewed life very differently, as far back as I can remember. I believe my brother was psychiatrically quite ill for most years of his adult life, but never got help for whatever his condition was, and I had no idea how deeply his problems ran. He showed cruelty towards animals like our pet dog Randy, who he'd kick and on one occasion tried to drown. Thank God I came on the scene just in time. He was physically aggressive towards people including me. He had also been placed in a Catholic orphanage, but a different one to mine. I think he was quite disturbed for a long time.

'Very early in his marriage, my brother became incredibly jealous and suspicious and started being violent towards Jenny, accusing her of having multiple affairs. He was drinking heavily but refused help. None of his accusations were true, but no matter what anyone said, he wouldn't budge in his thinking. Eventually he found his own sick solution. He and Jenny had three children between the ages of nine and four, two girls and a boy, and ... and...'

Jerome could see that Tom was becoming quite distressed. Jerome tried to settle Tom down, telling him they could continue later if he'd prefer. But Tom shook his head, and with his eyes on the ground he took a few deep breaths.

'It was about three-and-a-half years ago. One day Richard killed his three children. He had two girls aged nine and seven and a boy aged four.' Tom could not hold back sobs as he said his brother killed the girls by putting sedatives in their drinks, and then suffocating them.

'He took his young boy and drowned him in a bath. He had offered his wife Jenny a weekend away with Sue. Jenny returned home after the two days and found the bodies of her children. In addition to murdering his children, Richard had collected every photograph, and every bit of paper that had to do with the kids and set fire to it all. He was determined to remove any trace of the children's existence, as a way of punishing his wife. I had suspected for many years that he had some problems, but I had no idea that he could be psychotic.'

Tom's voice choked as he described Richard then killing himself and leaving Jenny to deal with it, as if anyone could deal with something so horrendous.

'She had a breakdown and was hospitalised in a psychiatric institution. This was in another town because she didn't want to see anything that reminded her of the past. As far as I know she's still there, without any improvement

Jenny has never wanted to see me, or anyone connected with Richard. I got the impression she was tarring me with the same brush, even though I have never been a violent person. It must have influenced my wife, too, because it was like she lost all trust in me.'

The hurt showed in Tom's face with his facial muscles acting in a manner no longer synchronised, creating a tight mask moistened by his tears. 'One day, Sue just walked out, taking our children with her: my son Luke, he was ten, and our daughter Primrose, two years older. She had no interest in counselling for us both, just broke off our marriage and refused to talk to me. I could never fathom whether she feared that I could become like my brother, or whether she could no longer live with someone who was genetically connected to the person who had caused the tragedy.

'So, in a flicker of time, I lost everything that was important to me, starting with my wife and children, and to a much lesser degree my brother, and essentially lost the prospect of a future. It felt like I was now labelled for the rest of my life as the brother of a child murderer.'

Tom was breathing heavily now, and his eyes glistened as he continually fought back tears.

'I was living close to a town called Guttenberg, in New Jersey. I used to work in law. I went to my GP, and we talked, and he believed I had become depressed. I was not suicidal, nor a danger to anyone else, but I really wanted to separate myself from the outside world. Given that Guttenberg is very densely populated, when my GP suggested getting treatment for my depression, I knew I had to get out of there if I wanted privacy. Otherwise, it would feel like I was living on top of a horde of people I knew and who knew me. So that's how I got here, and you know what Jerome, I don't want to leave. I don't want to be in that world outside without my wife and children, being constantly confronted with what happened with my brother. I understand you probably want to leave, and I don't mind helping you escape from here. But just as I understand what you feel you need, I hope you can understand why I don't want the same.

'When I think about it, it makes sense to me to hide from the trauma of that world outside. It's a world convulsing, with changes happening all the time, and not necessarily for the better in many cases. Sometimes it seems better, like lots of African countries gaining independence from European colonial rulers, but there are also these cold wars happening in Africa, Asia and Latin America. There's tension building up between the Soviet Union and most of the world, the assassination of Kennedy, the proxy war in Vietnam, and so it goes on. Man seems determined to destroy his planet.'

Tom was silent for a while, then he looked up and said in a soft voice, 'I wouldn't mind a drink after that. I guess I'll have to be content with a glass of water.' He sighed, then said: 'All right Jerome, it's your turn now. Tell me what brought you here and why you want to leave so much.'

Jerome felt overwhelmed by sorrow for what Tom had gone through. He knew that he also had experienced horror at times in his life, but what Tom described was so localised within the family that it must have been almost impossible to achieve any emotional distance from it. And although Jerome felt a remarkable closeness building between himself and Tom, hearing the history that Tom had just given, prompted a multitude of emotions and thoughts to surge through him. Jerome didn't feel ready to give his own history just yet.

'Tom, hearing your story has aroused a waterfall of emotions as if I could drown in the flood. Will you forgive me if we postpone it to tomorrow? Just so I can get my head around what I'm feeling.'

Tom with a gentle look on his face, said nothing but drew Jerome towards himself.

Jerome summed up his gratitude with one word. 'Thanks.'

Chapter 5

It was the third day of Jerome's stay in the ward, and he still hadn't heard from either Klein or Anderson. He'd expected one of them would visit him the evening before, but he'd been given some tablets which seemed to bomb him out, and he'd slept deeply.

He'd just woken up and still felt a bit groggy. Jerome wondered if the nurses had given him real medication, guessing they had. He felt giddy and was sure they had sedated him, with the same medicine they gave others in the ward, instead of the placebo his doctors would have planned to dispense to him. Uncomfortable with the anxiety that notion brought on, Jerome rapidly disposed of that unpleasant thought in the wastebasket of his mind, only to have it bounce back. He attempted to reassure himself with the belief that his doctors would certainly come and see him soon, but found those thoughts being rapidly discredited by his own mind. Deep down, he couldn't avoid the reality that kept intruding, telling him that wishes didn't come with guarantees.

After breakfast, Jerome and Tom joined six other patients who were seated on old metal chairs arranged in a circle in a small, bland room. This weekly get-together was called the 'Support Group', but according to Tom, despite its grand title, it did not aspire to provide support of any kind. Rather, it was essentially aimed at reminding patients about what was expected of them.

The group was run by Sister Rote. Jerome noted that her appearance – stiff white uniform, tightly bound upper body – had not altered in the slightest from when he'd last seen her. He decided to allow the mischievous side of himself to emerge, as a way of taking his mind off the troubling lack of contact with the two head psychiatrists. 'Matron,' he said, 'why is it that you have a uniform and none of the other staff do?'

Sister Rote glared at him for a few seconds, as if in two minds about whether she should brush him off or respond. The latter impulse won out. 'Why does it matter to you?' she practically snarled, her teeth bared like a guard dog.

Jerome, still wearing a slight smile, answered quietly, 'It matters to me because it baffles a lot of us, wondering who is staff and who isn't. I can see that it's very democratic having everyone dressed the same, in street clothes, but for people like us who are already stressed or sedated with medication, it can only cause confusion.'

Sister Rote stared at Jerome, her eyes piercing him, but she didn't respond verbally, seemingly letting that be her answer.

Jerome could see that Tom's hands were clenched in worry, but he persisted: 'I guess I'm also puzzled about why all the staff on the floor are male, except for yourself.'

A wave of giggles from the other patients carried across to the matron, who snapped with tight-lipped fury, 'That's enough.' When everyone had quietened, she continued: 'Who else has a question? A sensible question this time.'

Roger's voice now piped up: 'It puzzles me also.' It wasn't exactly a mutiny, but it was enough to stir the flames of the matron's anger. Jerome decided it was time to douse those flames by not provoking her further, hoping that she would not take out her ire on Roger later. He had been tempted to ask Sister Rote a further question regarding the racial issues apparent in the hospital's approach to staffing, but held back, having become aware of how stressed Tom appeared to become following the questions Jerome had previously raised. This reaction puzzled him, as he recalled Tom saying Sister Rote didn't scare him.

What pleased Jerome about all this, however, was seeing some semblance of interaction between the patients, some of the others laughing, and Roger's abrupt but supportive comment. Here in this group, Jerome felt relief as well as pleasure on detecting some interaction with the outside world. Probably not all of the group could do so, but at least some were starting to show signs of awareness of the world beyond.

Jerome decided to hold off doing or saying anything further that could possibly provoke Sister Rote. He had become increasingly aware that Sister Rote's power held sway in the ward he and Tom were housed in. Sure, Tom could say he wasn't scared of her, but she appeared to have the power to disrupt the life Tom had chosen to escape to. Dr. Klein had rejected the matron's suggestion that Tom would benefit from having electroconvulsive therapy, but maybe a time would come when he'd accept her idea. Jerome wondered whether thoughts like these eroded Tom's peace of mind.

After lunch, during which Tom remained relatively quiet, Jerome suggested they skip the occupational therapy session. He didn't think the staff would get too excited about their absence – they hadn't the previous day – and at worst they could use the excuse that they both had upset stomachs from lunch. Tom was agreeable to the idea and the two of them slipped away, heading back to the rough wooden bench they'd previously found.

For a short while they were both silent. Then Jerome coughed, looked down and readied himself to speak. He was ready to share more of his past with his friend. 'This is going to sound a bit like a B-grade movie …' he began, pausing when Tom gently reached out to let his hand rest on Jerome's shoulder.

Jerome wondered if his questioning of Sister Rote may have generated some ongoing concern in his new friend. Jerome like anyone else in that ward who was in touch with reality, had become aware of the matron's potential for vindictiveness. Why rock the boat if the matron's territory was intended to be your safe haven where you could hide from the tribulations of life?

Jerome broke the silence: 'I doubt that I can cover things in one go, but I guess I'll be here, in the hospital, for a while, so you'll eventually hear everything.' As he said this, in his private thoughts, he was certain – well, almost certain, that he would not be here that long, feeling amazed that it was taking some time for someone to question what the heck he was doing in Riverdale as a patient anyhow.

Jerome hesitated again, aware of forces pulling him in different directions. He wanted to confide in Tom, but confiding in people was not something he was used to doing. It felt to Jerome that doing so now might be symbolic of him accepting his fate, that he was stuck in this psychiatric ward, and he feared doing that. He didn't want to avoid life by remaining hospitalised, as Tom had chosen to do. He wondered if it would be smarter to just stop acting as a patient, otherwise both he and the people around him might start accepting that he belonged in this hospital. He was shocked by the idea of being trapped in the ward, unable to be discharged, but he was even more fearful of the possibility of passively deciding he was choosing to remain there, like Tom.

He had thought about this earlier and had managed to fence off the issues in different parts of his brain, to be dealt with later if need be. He knew that it was important for him to keep relating to those around him, but also that he might have to keep planning what was required to escape this ward. He clung to the hope that his predicament would be resolved by Klein or Anderson coming to see him soon, but he was so used to things going wrong in his life that even that thought could not be totally trusted.

Jerome realised Tom had been patiently waiting to hear what he had to say, so he now launched into his story: 'You know Tom, on the one hand, I feel dreadful not having memories a lot of the time. On the other hand, some of my memories are so painful that I wish I didn't have them. I sometimes question the point of having memories when I can only remember pain and horror, while at other times I reassure myself that there must have been good times, of love and warmth, especially with my mother, which I'm simply struggling to recall.'

As Tom gazed at him, Jerome continued in a gentle but strained voice: 'It may be hard for you to believe, but I can't remember the first five years of my life. However, I've managed to learn a lot about that period from other sources. Some of it was documented in official paperwork or told to me by family and close friends. Or I've filled in the gaps myself, knowing what happened to people trapped in similar situations.

'I believe that we tend to categorise people depending on the context in which we see them and how they appear to live. It's a really sore point for me that the way we perceive people is often so wrong.' The tension showed in Jerome's face as a faint smile struggled for position with the tight rod like features of the spasmodic muscles of anger, which won out and distorted his mouth.

He wiped his hand across his lips and looking down made himself continue.

'Tom, remember that speech I told you about when I got the medical school award? I tried to get them to see how unfair it is not to judge people by the personal qualities we see in the person, but rather judge them by some context which is not of their doing. If someone comes from a group of poor, disadvantaged people, then often they are assumed to be uneducated. Or if we see individuals who belong to a group of Catholic worshippers, we might question whether they could be potential molesters. And if we come across a group of Jewish people, there will be those who assume that some of those individuals must be money hungry. Or there's a group of women and you'll find some people assuming they are only interested in having babies and staying at home to do housework, or that they will be disinterested in sex.

'I know that is simplifying things, but I want to highlight how I think we are all guilty in varying degrees of putting people into categories and judging them according to those.' Jerome had a thought flash through his mind: *I'm in a psychiatric ward, so people will think I must be really crazy.* He decided he should keep that notion to himself.

'I learnt from my parents that I was born in Warsaw, Poland in 1941,' continued Jerome. 'It's hard to imagine anyone planning a pregnancy at the time, in that living hell. I've learnt from records in Washington's Holocaust Memorial Museum that I was arrested for the crime of being born to a Jewish mother. I was two weeks old at the time. My parents and I were imprisoned in a labour camp called Wolga Socolow, almost 50 kilometres from Warsaw. I am not sure why a baby was allowed to stay alive in that environment, as they would be useless for labour. After about nine months there, a policeman helped the three of us escape. Just why he did that, I was never told. I will probably never know. There were a few righteous people during that period, but the key word is "few". Another possibility that has hung about in my mind is that there usually was a price to be paid for freedom, and given that my mother was a very attractive woman…" His words disappeared and the meaningful silence hung in the air.

I can't help wondering when I came along. Was I really in that camp or was it after we escaped that I was born. I keep thinking how the Washington records were based on the history my parents gave.

'I don't blame my parents for not talking about it and I never pushed the point.' Jerome let the silence speak for itself without verbalising his suspicions.

'Back in Warsaw, my mother and I lived on false papers as gentiles, although I remember my mother saying she thought some people suspected we were Jewish but said nothing. My father lived separately from us, and I can't explain why. I was not told I was Jewish because I was only a child and might have blurted that out, which would have been a death sentence for all of us. So, I ran around with the other young hoods shouting the same antisemitic garbage. You can see how readily prejudice can be transmitted.'

Author is the child with wide hat sitting in middle of front row.
Neither he nor the other children aware he was Jewish. Popular with
many friends, yet if they knew he was Jewish they would have rejected
him, so becoming an outcast and he probably would have been killed.
Yet he was the same child they once liked.

Jerome was quiet for a while, his moist eyes fixed on the ground near his feet.

'There are many unanswered questions in my mind that I can only guess the answers to. Like why on earth would my parents have me circumcised, as in Poland at that time it was diagnostic of being Jewish and an automatic death sentence? Not long after, my parents corrected the situation, with a Jewish doctor in the Warsaw ghetto performing a procedure on me, as if restoring my virginity.

'There are a lot of blind spots in my memory regarding that period, where my understanding and recall of events is limited or confused. In many ways, it is probably better that I leave those unknowns as they are. Some questions are better not answered, like what price had to be paid to secure my family's temporary freedom. Especially my mother's possible role in it. I often think about what would be worse – having the memory or guessing the truth. What I do know is that the experiences of that time damaged my parents for life, and I've also come around to the idea that the next generation, like myself, was also damaged. We're alive, and hopefully aware of the overwhelming importance of treating other people well. But if I allow it, it gets me down when I start dwelling on the fact that, apart from the evil of millions of people being cruelly slaughtered based on race and religion, many of those people would have gone on to have children if they'd remained alive. Thus, their murder killed the potential for a multitude of future lives.

'I occasionally have dreams of black smoke billowing from the chimneys of crematoria, and piles of gold fillings that have been taken from corpses, and people of all ages screaming as they are gassed and burnt to death. Onlookers in these dreams laugh as they watch the show. The unremitting sadism and cruelty that happened during the years of the Holocaust is unbearable to think about. Sounds, screams and visions pollute the air. Seeing small bodies turned into wreaths of smoke, contaminating a silent blue sky.

'I've thought a lot about evil over the years and how it seems to me that animals don't kill out of sadistic pleasure but only for food or to protect themselves, and yet we humans see ourselves as a superior species.'

Jerome confessed that he continued to be horrified by the knowledge that it wasn't only the German Nazis who'd carried out the slaughter of Jews. There were many individuals in many European countries who gladly assisted in rounding up innocent people, mostly Jews of all ages, who were then transferred to extermination camps. They also took gypsies and people with psychiatric disorders, deeming them unfit to live. Some of the individuals assisting the slaughter of adults and children may have joined out of fear, others may have joined in the killing hoping to gain jobs and property, and some because they identified with the Nazis and had similar beliefs about Jews.

'You know, Tom,' said Jerome, 'I've seen the phrase *banality of evil*, and somehow it seems a ridiculous term to me. There is nothing banal or common about sadistic killers, yet there have been times when doctors might have killed their former patients, teachers might have killed their former pupils, and so on. It may just be possible that any person can do evil things depending on the circumstances and what they have been taught. It's a horrible thought, but are we all potentially capable of doing evil things depending on the events we're caught up in?' Jerome looked at Tom and their eyes locked sharing the sadness they were feeling, and a gentle smile on Tom's features reached out to support Jerome.

Jerome was providing a frank, open history of himself, just as Tom had the previous day. He was aware of a torrent of thoughts and emotions building up but was determined to keep it all under control.

Suddenly, Carlos appeared, jogging towards them. 'Sorry guys,' he said, 'but Sister Rote feels you're missing too many things the hospital has set up. She wants to see you now.'

Jerome waved him away. 'Just say you couldn't find us, and I promise you we'll be back in a half-hour or so.' But Carlos shook his head and started to move off. To Jerome's surprise, Tom had already gotten up and quickly followed Carlos. Jerome, controlling his frustration, did the same, puzzled why Sister Rote had such a strong hold on Tom. He suspected the explanation he'd come up with earlier that day might well explain it. The matron was a powerful, angry woman who could be vindictive if provoked. Tom had escaped from the stress of life outside and saw the matron as a possible source of ongoing pain in his new haven.

Tom and Jerome re-entered the hospital, and Carlos guided them to the matron's office before darting away. They found her standing at the door, glaring. She barked at them to 'Sit down!' pointing at the two chairs that were in front of her meticulously tidy desk.

Jerome and Tom did as they were told, as Sister Rote walked behind her desk, to where she could now tower over them.

Her words hissed towards them: 'I think you are both sicker than the doctors realise, and I'll need to fill them in. It's too late for activities; go rest in your room and stay there. I don't want you going anywhere else.'

As they walked towards their room, Jerome realised he was itching to reveal more to his friend. He had to get it out now, or he was afraid he might never do it. So, when they reached their ward, he looked at Tom and said in a voice just above a whisper, 'You know even better than me, in here people don't intrude and we can speak privately. Are you okay with that? There's a bit more I'd like to tell you.' Jerome took Tom's smile as agreement, and he said, 'Thanks.'

The two men settled on to their beds as Jerome went on: 'Tom, you may not think so, but there are a lot of similarities between the pressures that you and I have both had to deal with over the years.' As Jerome caught his breath and attempted to let some calm in, he glanced around the ward. He saw five other men nearby either lying on their beds or sitting on chairs next to the beds.

It was as he predicted. There was no interaction between the other patient group and Tom and Jerome, no speech or any other sound. The sounds would erupt under cover of darkness as they slept. For the moment they lived in separate worlds. Jerome guessed that if anything caught the attention of the other patients in his ward whilst awake, it would not be anything Jerome noticed himself. Physically, he believed they could sit side by side on the same bench and yet be occupying separate worlds.

He guessed - no, he believed - these men in his ward were regularly bombarded by images and sounds coming from within them that he was not privy to. They had no urge to share these sensations, but regardless of whether they wanted to share or not, the other night demonstrated how it was out of their control. In the blackness of night, the uncontrolled army of sights and sounds took over and the screams of fear from its victims poured out. They were shared, but not by choice.

As Jerome anticipated, Tom and he occupied another world and Jerome could talk in private as if no-one else was there.

Jerome then looked towards Tom, who remained silent, but his face reflected a mix of intense interest and sadness. Jerome paused to take in this image and then continued: 'Somehow, each stage of my life has had challenges. I've managed to overcome them, but I'm getting tired of needing to fight each step of the way.'

With the declaration of these conflicts, Jerome's voice became louder and pressured, so that his words were spat out like sparks from a firecracker. Even though he knew he should be more discreet and calmer, he found he couldn't help it. He began stuttering and his face was flushed, as rivulets of moisture trickled to the ground.

Jerome forced out more words to describe what he felt: 'I'm tired of carrying secrets, that I'm Jewish, that my parents were alcoholics, and so on. I'm sick of people not bothering to get to know me but rather judging me against things that have nothing to do with me as a person. Being Jewish, having parents who were alcoholics, none of that defines the person I am.'

Suddenly, Carlos wandered in, causing Jerome to quickly stop his confession. 'Everything OK guys?' said the nursing aide with a grin. Jerome wasn't sure to what extent he could trust any of the staff who worked in the ward. However, Carlos did appear different in that he would smile and laugh and interact with the patients in the ward. Clearly referring to Sister Rote, Carlos added: 'Once that battle axe gets going, you can't rein her in. Just pretend you go along with it.'

With his head down, Carlos sauntered back towards the door, but before he reached it, he turned and grinned, looking straight at Jerome: 'We right for that arm-wrestle tonight?'

'Sure,' replied Jerome. 'We can work out the odds and the money later.' They had done some arm-wrestling since Jerome's admission to the ward. Part of it seemed related to Carlos hoping to be paid for winning, but Jerome wondered if there was any other motivation. So far, they had competed on four occasions, with Carlos the victor on three of them. Sometimes the arm of Carlos slipped towards the groin area of his opponent and lingered there, but nothing more.

As soon as Carlos had left, Jerome went on, more subdued this time: 'I've probably told you about our escape from the camp and the possible price that had to be paid for that. We were helped to escape and learnt later that about two months after our escape the camp was destroyed, and all its inhabitants killed.' Looking down at his feet, in a flat angry monotone Jerome continued 'Words can't really describe it, but we survived the massacre of the Holocaust, although the damage it caused to my parents never went away.'

'I told you it was a policeman who helped us escape.' This wasn't an ordinary policeman but the local police chief. Jerome said he wasn't told any more about this by his parents, but he was sure that assistance like that came at a price.

Looking straight into Tom's eyes somewhat defiantly, 'Like I said before, my mother was a very attractive woman. Whilst I can't help thinking, I don't want to know any more and wouldn't judge her if she did sacrifice herself to save our lives'.

With moist downcast eyes Jerome said, 'I know who my mother was, and I don't need to know more.'

Jerome described his parents and himself escaping to Paris as the Russian forces approached Poland and from Paris escaping to Birmingham in a somewhat decrepit boat.

In a defiant tone of voice he added, 'Decrepit it might have been, but it stayed afloat, and we made it. We made it, but the three of us were damaged and it destroyed my parent's marriage.'.

'There's a saying that captures that damage, I feel: "Suspicion crowds the vessel in which it resides, leaving little room for love, trust or any other positive emotion.'

'So, while we all survived, we missed out in other ways.

Not sure why they chose that place Birmingham, maybe just because they had to run somewhere, away from those killing fields, leaving the bodies of friends and relatives piled up or already buried or just as scattered ashes.'

Jerome, the blood now drained from his face, described how, the night before last, he'd felt as if he was choking, breathless, as if air was being sucked out him. He was enveloped by an impure, dirty sound, a kind of scream, a harbourer of problems that could not be escaped. Such nights only occurred infrequently even before his hospital admission, but when they occurred, they took their toll.

Forcing himself to put the nightmares to one side, Jerome started talking about his family's arrival in England: 'The immigration official dealing with us asked some questions,' he said, 'but when he could see that we couldn't speak English very well, he just finished up the interview, saying, "You'll be right." Almost on the spot, my parents decided Wright would be our new surname, so I became Brian Wright.'

A smile brightened Jerome's face. 'I've always wondered whether that name appealed to 'my parents because it didn't sound Jewish.' He sighed, then said: 'There were so many things I was uncertain about regarding that period of time.

'I had trouble over the years knowing whether I was entitled to be angry with my parents when they annoyed me or whether I had to make allowances for how they were behaving because of their own damage from the war.' Jerome now looked directly into Tom's eyes. 'Do you know what the Nazi leadership spoke about? They visualised eliminating all the Jews in the world and one day having a museum for an extinct race. It would contain reminders of the race that no longer existed. We would've been just an exhibit of something that no longer existed, like the dodo.'

Jerome shivered drawing a deep breath. 'School in Birmingham was difficult for me at first because I was different and being different makes you the focus of bullying. It's the last thing a young child wants. I couldn't speak English but learned in a hurry. Still, I was dressed differently, and the food that I took to school was foreign. I remained this way for quite a few years when all I wanted was to be the same as everyone else.

'When I say it was difficult, that word doesn't do it justice. I quickly became a social outcast, unwelcome in the homes of the other kids. And it wasn't just because I was different, but because of my parents too. Sometimes a new kid started at the school and if they showed an inclination to interact with me, to get to know me, hands would reach out and pull them away. "You don't want to go there," they'd be told. "They're alcoholic bums." These accusations felt like sledgehammers battering my body.

'I avoided public urinals, which at first was a mystery even to me. But it was because of the circumcision. Even though I'd had that procedure in Warsaw, it had been ingrained in me when I was younger to avoid any kind of public exposure of my genitals. I only went in cubicles, like at school. Anyway, there was one occasion when this all turned out to be humiliating. It was the end of the school day and, well, I needed a piss. I'd gone to the school toilets, but all the cubicles were occupied, so I decided to catch a tram and go home as quick as I could, rather than go to a public urinal. As I waited at the tram stop, as more and more kids were arriving, I felt a trickle finding a path down both legs. The trickle became a stream, enveloping my lower half in fluid, as dark patches flagged my loss of control. The indifference shown to me by the other kids was now replaced by a savage mockery, leaving me practically swimming in my bodily fluids. It was yet again a reminder that what was on offer was not friendship. Over and over, it was conveyed to me that my family and I were despised.

'There were a few other boys who also didn't belong, and I formed friendships with some of them. But I'm ashamed to remember that at times I remained silent or even joined in a bit when some other kid was being bullied, say for being gay. When the cry 'backs to the wall' would ring out. I didn't do much to them, but I also didn't try to befriend or defend them.

'Also, there were a few girls on the fringe because their parents were poor, or coloured, or somehow not part of the establishment. I had some dates with several of them – nothing serious, but it provided some sexual relief. I'm embarrassed to say I can't recall their names. I had the crazy idea that decent girls didn't enjoy sex, and if a girl did seem to like sex, then there was something cheap about her. It's a belief I can't shake off even now.' He paused before adding: 'A few times when I was older, I frequented a brothel, and later felt ashamed of what was happening to those young girls.'

Jerome told Tom yet again how he had become increasingly aware that things were missing in his life. Many of the kids had grandparents, and on the weekends they would all get together, in a warm atmosphere. In subdued tones, looking at the ground, Jerome said, 'I lost most of my extended family during the Holocaust, but at first, I did not know people were missing. I guess I've told you that, but these thoughts rotate in my brain and the only relief is to get them out. Only gradually, when I started looking around, I could see what other kids had as distinct to what I had. I was surrounded by gaps rather than family and these were gaps that could never be filled'.

Jerome wondered if this was too much too quickly for Tom to absorb but was encouraged by the gentle smile and strong attention he sensed coming from Jerome.

Yet again with moist eyes and tight voice Jerome enquired whether Tom wanted a break and continue later, say tomorrow.

Tom didn't use words but the gentle look on his face and the firm touch of his hand which reached out and stroked Jerome's right shoulder, was sufficient to open the gates, encouraging Jerome to continue.

Jerome restrained his tears and spoke in a rapid voice. 'I'm sure all this can happen in just about every country in the world.' The pressured words were emitted without any hint of doubt.

Jerome was quiet for a short while, and not only held his voice in but his breath as well. Nothing moved.

Looking down, in a monotone, Jerome continued. We escaped the brutality of Europe, but cruelty comes in many shapes. I began living in so called *freedom* and going to school. And what do you think happened? I was not allowed to forget that I was Jewish, or to be comfortable with it. I was called many names, except my real one. Called *kike* and *dago*, and kids made up creative little rhymes: "To market to market to buy a fat pig; home again, home again, jiggety jig." They'd yell, '*Go back to where you came from, Jew.*'

Still looking down and speaking like a jet of water squirted from a hose, 'There's a memory that continues to hurt and anger me. It really pisses me off. I was in a bus going to school and as I went to pay for my ticket, handing over the coins the bitch of a conductress greeted me with "Robbed the synagogue money box, have you?" I wanted to yell at her, but what came were tears flooding down my face. I hated knowing that my reaction was giving people like her pleasure. I fought but failed to hold my tears back. I couldn't help being aware I was on my own-and under attack yet again. No one stood up for me and in fact, I sensed a few of the kids edging away.

'I could never make out what was wrong with being different. I could say my name was Wright, but to them I was still Sokonovsky.

'I did well in school, and gradually became more and more like the people around me. However, inside I knew I was different, and so did the townspeople. My family had reached safety, but I was bullied mercilessly. A stranger in paradise! I fantasised about getting my revenge on the bullies, but being fantasies, they gradually evaporated.

To survive, I learnt when to move and when to stay still, to be inconspicuous. There was no one I could think of that I could ask for protection. The teachers did nothing to help, nor did my parents, my mother too deflated, my father too ill and then my stepfather not giving a damn.

'Away from school, there were moments of peace and wonderment and magic. I would wake up after a night's sleep, lie there and see the early rays of the sun shining on the garden as if a spaceship was descending. After a while I came to believe that this pattern of light was a harbinger of good fortune, but deep down I knew it was only an indicator of warm weather. Whatever – having it occur was as close to happiness as anything I could achieve in those days.

What was missing, though, was highlighted every Sunday when my parents and I would regularly visit this Jewish home. It belonged to the grandparents of a couple that my mother had come to know. I think their name was Wynn, and the grandparents were these two little gentle people who sat on their couch smiling away, not saying much but surrounded by a horde of their children and grandchildren. The house seemed to be filled with happy noise and affection. I loved being there, but it was bittersweet, as it showed clearly what was absent in our family life.'

Jerome abruptly changed focus, pushing yet again into the worst of his story: 'My father's belief in God ceased when he died from heart failure, when I was about eight years of age. I found it difficult to understand how my father had continued to believe in a god despite what he'd experienced and witnessed during those horrific times of the Holocaust. Maybe the only way he could deal with all that horror was to view it as part of some mysterious plan created by an all-powerful entity, and not just as the roll of the dice. It feels scary for many people to think that the sequence of life is that we are born and eventually, one day, we die, and what happens in-between depends on us and chance. It is comforting to believe there is some powerful higher being who monitors and controls what goes on in the world and looks after us. *If only*, I thought to myself in private. The Holocaust alone disproved that theory.

'When my father died, my mother, in her insecurity, rushed into a marriage with a man who turned out to be a violent alcoholic. My stepfather bashed my mother regularly and at times would belt me also. Other people wanted nothing to do with our family; they certainly wouldn't allow their children to have much to do with me. I must have loved my mother when I was younger, as I was aware of having ongoing warm feelings towards her, but I can't recall how she was back then.'

During this torrent of emotions Tom had moved inconspicuously and sat quietly with his right arm around Jerome.

Almost whispering, Jerome spoke as if in a daze.

'The first memory I have of her, my mum, is a person who had lost all zest for life. Her personality had been stripped from her by the losses of the war years and then by the brutality of her second husband. When I was about fifteen, my mother finally found escape from her years of misery by taking her life with an overdose of tablets. In reality, I had lost her years before, when she withdrew and stopped being the bubbly, fun-loving person that she apparently once was, from the descriptions of people who knew her back then.

'I can't recall that person, but I knew I had loved her: no, we loved each other. The warmth I felt for her didn't come out of nowhere.'

Jerome became silent, shackled by his emotions. Tom quietly encouraged him to go on.

His voice fighting against the resistance of his emotions, in a sound so fragmented and pressured that he could not recognise it, Jerome forced himself to go on. 'A couple of months before my mother ended her own life, I heard muffled screams from her bedroom. I couldn't stop myself. As I pushed open her bedroom door, I could hear her whimpering. The light I flicked on showed the punching bag of misery that was my mother. My stepfather snarled, 'Get the fuck out of here you little turd.' I was working out by then, so I was well built. I feared my stepfather, but I was full of rage at what he was doing to my mother. I'm glad that my anger won out over my fear.'

Almost hissing, the anger breaking through, Jerome spat out: 'He – no, I can't bring myself to refer to him by name – he jumped out of bed stark-naked, and we stood there glaring at each other. I was shaking, partly with fear as he was a big violent man, but with age and too much grog, his body just hung on him. I kicked his balls. He doubled over and I kicked him again in the backside and punched him in the head as he fell to the ground. My mother was still whimpering, and as I looked at the two them it felt like it was a junkyard of wasted souls.

I decided right then that I was moving out and tried to persuade my mother to join me. But after what she'd gone through with the Holocaust, then losing her husband and finally living with that drunken brute, she was resigned to a life of …of…' His voice broke. 'To a life of not living. She wouldn't come with me…stayed on … escaped with… with pills… a whole bottle of them. Swallowed them a couple of months after I left'

His thoughts found residence in silence. Tom hugged him and like statues they held each other up.

Jerome continued. 'I blamed myself… no I didn't. I did and I didn't, his voice sobbed. I told myself she'd died years before I left, but I knew my leaving was probably the full stop ending her years of misery. Sometimes when I'm down, really down, I can't help thinking she might have lived on if I hadn't moved out.

Still holding each other, Jerome whispered. 'After that fight with my stepfather, I spent my first night sleeping under a bridge. I went to live with a paternal aunt. I didn't really know Aunt Lois – she was elderly, single, caring enough to take me in, but not able to do much more. I thought I'd drop out of school, but my aunt, she reminded me I needed school if I wanted a job.

'I could never forget those years at home. My schoolmates never allowed me to forget the home they said I came from.'

Jerome, his face soaked in tears, which in turn-soaked Tom's hands, slumped down onto his bed and turned away, needing some time to escape on his own.

Physically his body separated from Tom, but his mind found no rest, and the pain he had just shared with Tom, swirled around in his head.

Tom silently watched over him and then respected Jerome's need for a period of silence but maintained a vigil over him. Tom stayed in his own bed but rolled over, granting Jerome the illusion of privacy that he sought.

Jerome found himself thinking about the personal history he had just shared with Tom, seeking other memories that he had avoided facing for too long. He began reflecting some more on his relationship with his mother and others in the family. He couldn't clearly recall his mother, but he had a faint awareness of tangled fibres of warmth and laughter that tied him to her memory. He believed this fitted in with what he had been told by other people who'd known his mother and described how she had adored him. That would explain the strong feelings of affection that he still had towards her.

He started pondering what her marriage to his father was like, before reminding himself that he was not a hundred per cent sure that the man was actually his father, recalling how dismissive the man had been of the young Jerome. It really hurt him to think about this, which was partly why he'd decided to relegate the idea to the garbage bin of history. It was difficult for him not to think about it every waking hour, but he was determined not to live in the shadow of his parents forever. He had resolved that he would allow the doubt about who his father was, that huge question, to remain unanswered. There were some things that were better not discovered. The feelings that bound him to inaction were very strong. He had no doubts who mothered him-that would be enough.

One more memory came to him. His mother had a rag doll that was given to her when she was only a few years old. It had bits missing from it, like one eye, but she adored it and would hug it for comfort and take it to bed, even as an adult. After she died, he'd reclaimed the doll and buried it. It seemed unfair that the doll should live longer than she had.

Chapter 6

DAY FOUR

Once again, Jerome woke up feeling bombed out from the medication Bitterly he thought-'they call this treatment'. He was frightened, as the medication from the night before diminished his feeling of being in control.

It also seemed unbelievable to him that no-one had cottoned on to the fact that he was not genuinely ill and didn't require hospitalisation. There was no limit to the thoughts flooding his mind, but none of the thoughts could open locked doors. He found it amazing that trained psychiatric staff could fail to detect that he didn't belong in a psychiatric ward, yet no-one had voiced that reality, and the reality was becoming engulfed by a nightmare.

Jerome was increasingly aware that his thoughts were racing in many directions, as if desperate to escape the enclosure holding them. He wished he had Tom's calm but realised he in fact feared being at ease with the notion of making a psychiatric ward his long-term home. Jerome knew he had to regain control of his thoughts, emotions, and actions to have any chance of creating a meaningful life outside the hospital.

As he lay in bed, the stress he felt brought back the mixture of confusion and bitterness that had overwhelmed him when his mother died. He realised, all these years later, he was still going in circles, immersed in both anger and helplessness, wanting to change something that was so very wrong but was now beyond repair. Grieving for his mother continued to be difficult as he could not avoid thinking about her life of suffering. Jerome felt crushed when he contemplated how her life had been ravaged by one person or another – until she escaped by ending it. He continued to feel that his leaving home had added to her determination to end it all.

His mind veered to something else that was troubling him intensely. He had realised that whilst he had been in this current ward, there had been no sign of anyone being discharged, or of planning for a discharge, or even evidence of anyone being allowed to leave. It felt like all the patients were there for life. Even Tom, currently sleeping in the next bed, had been there for two years without any talk of exiting the facility. But he knew Tom had no desire to leave; the hospital ward was the home Tom had chosen for the future.

After fully rousing themselves, Jerome and Tom went to the dining area and ate their breakfasts in silence. They then walked back through the grounds to their decrepit wooden bench. The heavy sound of silence surrounded them. There were no activities scheduled for this morning, so they knew they wouldn't get in trouble with Sister Rote.

There was a mutual sense of trust and caring that drew them to each other. Tom quietly allowed Jerome to share thoughts and emotions that he would never divulge to others. Jerome put into words the feeling that wouldn't leave him. His voice soft but intense like the crack of a whip told Tom that he found it incredible that none of the staff had picked up on him not needing to be there. He didn't conceal his agitation and felt the pain building up in his forehead, as moisture caused his undershirt to cling to his body. Tom reached out and with his arm drew Jerome to himself. Gradually the waves of tension settled, and Jerome shared with Tom the prophesy that it would all improve further with Dr. Klein coming that evening. Jerome was aware as he spoke, how strange his thoughts must sound to Tom, who he felt was still unaware of the reasons for Jerome being hospitalised in a psychiatric ward, though he had initially attempted to fill him in. At the time he described the background of Klein and Anderson setting up a research project and making Jerome an irresistible offer. His words ran for cover as he became increasingly aware that Tom was only listening out of politeness. It began sounding like a fantasy even to himself. To be continued was the exit strategy.

Once again, Jerome confided to Tom how impressed he was with Tom's calm and ability to handle anger and stress in contrast to Jerome himself, who was struggling with these negative emotions. Jerome gave a bitter laugh as he remarked that bottled up anger was just what a psychiatrist needed. Jerome sensed that Tom continued to disbelief that Jerome had trained as a medical doctor and was now looking to train further in psychiatry. Despite those apparent doubts, there was still some factor that generated empathy for each other and the feeling they shared something that drew them to each other.

Jerome had initially attempted to fill in some of the gaps in his personal history and clarified that there were many key events he personally could not recall, and documentations he could not find. Some events were described in paperwork he had accessed, but there was so much pain and horror associated that he chose not to discuss it at this stage

In a very soft voice, almost a whisper, Jerome confided that there were so many things that were horrendous and designated at home as 'not for discussion', it made it feel as if his life history was made up of deep excavations creating dungeons where horror was stored.

Jerome, his voice weighed down with doubt tried to further explain 'It created the feelings, doubts like I had huge gaps of life that never really existed, except in my mind.' He confided that it made him feel at times that his life rhythm was destroyed, and occasionally it felt as if he was depositing large slices of life in a storage that he could never access. It made it difficult to decide what was real and what wasn't, in his life — as if his own life didn't exist or was a figment of his imagination. It was hard at times to separate what he'd experienced, what had been told to him and what he imagined. A lot of what he visualised was like a film projected from learning about people in similar circumstances and what they had experienced. Not speaking about it to anyone else in the past added to the feeling of unreality.

He breathed deeply, then began speaking rapidly, afraid he might soon reach the limit of Tom's patience with these conversations: 'I was invited about four years back to join a group intending to visit Poland, hoping to gauge where the members of the group, who were all Jewish, where if anywhere did they fit into the modern version of that country. I turned down the offer as I had strong doubts that Poland wanted me as an equal, and in turn, I doubted I could ever forgive what many of its citizens had done during the Holocaust. It troubles and angers me that Poland has never been prepared to examine and own up to a significant degree of complicity in assisting the Nazis in rounding up and killing Jews.' Unlike Germany, there is no evidence at a government level that any significant effort is being made to educate young Poles as to what happened during the horror of the Holocaust.'

'I've read documentation that appeared reliable, how even after the Germans were defeated, the Poles killed thousands of Jews who had come to retrieve their homes and belongings. The Polish

Government has never acknowledged this. This lack of recognition of how badly some Poles behaved towards their Jewish neighbours has prevented young poles learning from history.'

I can't avoid thinking that with this approach the risk of a new generation of young Poles growing up prejudiced might be really high. What prevents them developing the same hatred as their parents before them.?

In an intense voice, Jerome added: 'But then, how many countries in Europe did act well. As it is said, evil occurs when people, good people, stand by and do nothing. However, I have also thought about the brave Poles who risked their lives to protect and save Jews. They were admirable, courageous, but small in number.'

Jerome looked at Tom trying to gauge his reaction. He put this query to Tom, asking whether the discussion had become too intense and too prolonged for him. Tom gently said he appreciated Jerome sharing something so close to himself, experiences and emotions that were important, and he, Tom, wanted to hear as much as Jerome was comfortable in sharing.

Feeling partly reassured, as he didn't know whether Tom was just being kind to him, Jerome went on. 'I feel concerned that the Holocaust has become an obsession that might only damage me further. Of course, I won't ever forget it, but I want to use that knowledge in a positive way to make me more sensitive to how I treat other people, and to remind me to be supportive of people in need. I don't want to live the life of a victim consumed with grief and anger and allow this to poison my relationships. There will always be some sadness and anger about what occurred and what I lost, but I need to get this translated into something that helps me care for other people in a constructive way. At the same time, it is a lesson in history that should never be allowed to be forgotten or distorted, so people can be more aware of the dark road that prejudice can lead them down.'

The horrifying figure that had stuck in Jerome's mind time and again was that in 1939, the population of Poland was about 35 million people, with approximately three million of these beings Jews. Ninety per cent of that Jewish population was murdered, with a significant part of the Polish population assisting in the carnage, or merely standing by and allowing it to happen. He acknowledged it would have taken immense courage to actively oppose the carnage.

Jerome lifted his head and looked at Tom. 'I'm sorry if that's getting too heavy Tom,' he said.

Tom smiled gently. 'You've got nothing to be sorry about Jerome. What you're saying makes sense to me and it's got me thinking.'

'Thanks,' said Jerome, getting up from the bench. 'Let's take a walk - get it out of our system.'

They strolled quietly, allowing the sunlight dancing on the stream to calm them both. Briefly, they stopped and watched several butterflies fluttering amongst the swamp milkweed, while a gentle breeze caressed their cheeks. For that short period of time, all felt right with the world.

As they continued walking through the hospital's grounds, Tom said, 'I read somewhere that Abraham Lincoln had a saying: It's not the years of life but the life in your years that counts.'

Jerome pondered this as the two men continued to walk aimlessly. He reconsidered his belief that to live well, people require not only a future but also a past – both are needed to make a person feel real, that they exist.

His thoughts then returned to how many people take up religion to help them deal with the fear and anxiety of nothingness. Religion provided a kindly superior being in charge of life events, looking after you, otherwise what happened in a person's life depended on their own actions and the roll of the dice.

What was his own path, Jerome thought to himself. In the ward, he didn't seem to be directing his life. Instead, he constantly felt ripples of tension, yet certain it was only a matter of time before someone confronted him about what he was doing in Riverdale. And underneath that thought festered another concern. What if he got to like being a patient and didn't want to leave, like Tom? He wanted to dismiss this concern as ludicrous, but it continued to hang around in the back of his mind.

One thing of which there was no doubt was that the closeness between Jerome and Tom was much, much more than Jerome had ever achieved with people on the 'outside'. He wondered whether he and Tom could ever have a relationship external to the hospital, but concluded that it was unlikely, given Jerome's determination to escape and Tom's wish to stay.

Jerome found the ward unbearable at times. What impacted most on him in that soulless room was the feeling that eyes dominated, not by looking at anyone but by gazing inwards, totally preoccupied with inner thoughts, reflecting the damaged souls that resided there. Eyes were apparently the window to the soul, but in the ward, it felt as if the blinds on those windows had been drawn. One could no longer look into those eyes, and Jerome doubted whether those eyes could look out.

As the two men turned back towards the hospital's main building, Jerome recalled how, whilst shaving that morning, he had carefully checked himself in the mirror, seeking reassurance that his eyes differed from those around him. What he saw were eyes capable of tears, and with the ability to see other people, but they also had dilated pupils, reflecting his anxiety. He began wondering, with not a little trepidation, about the risk that being hospitalised for a long period at Riverdale would cause him to look like the other patients. The thought that he might want to stay so that he could escape the pressures of life by taking on the role of patient, frightened him.

Still, being in the presence of Tom, a person more like himself, gave him some reassurance. Indeed, he had been experiencing increasingly warm feelings towards Tom. In spite of that a bitter question hit him. Why was it that the more he cared for or valued a relationship, the more likely he was to run the risk of losing it? He found himself intermittently checking Tom's reactions to reassure himself the positive feelings remained mutual.

Later that day, whilst making plaster moulds and drawing with crayons in the same grey, soulless room where he ate his meals, Jerome found himself continuing to fantasise that, at any moment, someone would tap him on the shoulder and accuse him of being a fraud, not a real patient. He wondered how many of the other patients were so withdrawn that they were oblivious of him, or whether some of them had noted a difference between themselves and him.

He also felt uncomfortable thinking about how much more anger he was storing up inside himself compared to Tom. Even though he could acknowledge the stress he had experienced over the years, it troubled him that he carried that level of rage and self-pity at times. He couldn't avoid thinking of his life as being dominated by a series of battles and crises that he'd had to overcome. And yes, he had won those battles, so far at least, but he wondered at what cost.

There was always an aspect of his life where part of it was hidden, and he'd never felt free to be totally up-front with the truth. There had always been something to hide, and he craved the courage and freedom that would grant him the ability to be himself.

He had now told Tom a lot about the pressures he'd felt in his life, including having his family decimated during the Holocaust, losing people whose faces he could no longer recall, and for whom there wasn't even a photo or grave to remember them by. He'd also explained how, for far too much of his life, he felt he'd been judged by factors that had little or nothing to do with him personally. He suddenly recalled another story to do with how a person perceives other people.

The famous scientist Albert Einstein was doing a circuit of American universities, giving a series of talks, when he found himself wishing that he could get back to the laboratory and continue his work. One evening, as he was being driven to yet another talk by his chauffeur, Felix, he expressed this wish to return to the lab.

Felix laughed and said, 'I've got an idea boss. I've heard you give this talk so many times, I bet I could give it for you.'

Felix pointed out that he also physically resembled Einstein to a significant degree, so the ruse had a good chance of working.

Now it was Einstein's turn to laugh. He was tickled by the idea and said, 'Why not? Let's give it a go.'

When they arrived at the presentation, Einstein, who had donned his chauffeur's cap and jacket, sat at the back of the room while Felix got up on stage and took the microphone. Einstein's chauffeur then confidently gave the talk that the scientist himself usually gave. He even answered several questions from the audience, quite expertly. Then, towards the end of the session, a pompous professor stood up and asked a very esoteric question.

Without missing a beat, Felix fixed the professor with a steely stare and said, 'Sir, the answer to your question is so simple that I'll let my chauffeur, who is sitting up at the back, answer it for me.'

Jerome understood that the story might be true, but apocryphal or not, it still highlighted how a person could be perceived entirely by their name, their reputation, and what others had said about them. Jerome may well have topped his medical class and had a lot of positive personal qualities, but to many, that meant far less than the fact that he was the son of two alcoholic bums. Most people had never responded to him based on the person he was.

Jerome recalled an old Indian proverb that described how an army of tigers led by a sheep would always lose to an army of sheep led by a tiger. He wasn't sure what brought it to mind except the thought that he had to be responsible for himself.

These musings were pushed away by a rising concern, verging on panic, at not having heard from Klein or Anderson yet. All day, staff had fobbed off his queries as to when Klein's presence was expected, although there had been the hint of someone attending to him that very night. Then there was the impact of the tablets the staff had given him the previous two nights. He imagined that getting medication like that each evening could well cause him to present less human like the other people in the ward. He now also understood more clearly that the men around him in the ward were damaged human beings who had likely been further impaired by a lack of adequate therapy, with little to no communication with staff, and no attention. Instead, the hospital's approach appeared to be a custodial one, where everyone was managed in the same way regardless of their condition, with the sole aim of maintaining order, getting everyone to follow the directions of staff. Both staff and patients had given up any expectation of improvement.

As Jerome struggled to keep his panic under control, he tried to fix his mind on the outcome he wanted. This evening, he hoped – no, not hoped, he would demand – that Dr. Klein or Dr. Anderson come to see him.

O

As the clock on the wall of the ward ticked past 6 pm, Jerome sat on his bed, the curtains drawn all the way around it, with only one thought on his mind. It had to be Dr. Klein coming to see him, as they'd arranged. He was desperate for this to be the case. He felt washed out from the anxiety and stress he had experienced during the day, and he couldn't shake the sedating impact of the tablets he'd been given.

Abruptly, a small, thin face poked through the curtains, a visage that was soon revealed to be connected to a stick-like body that seemed to hop rather than walk. Jerome had difficulty accepting the strange figure, which reminded him of an enormous praying mantis. This man was unlike anyone he'd ever seen before, and it was certainly not a reassuring substitute for Dr. Klein. A piercing pain shot through Jerome's head as his confusion spiked.

The bizarre entity had to be a doctor, as he had a stethoscope around his neck, but why had he called on Jerome in place of Klein, or Anderson? Who was he? Were the psychiatrists' playing games with him?

The thin and reedy voice emitted by the figure seemed to match the man's physical presentation.

'You were probably expecting Dr. Klein,' said Praying Mantis, 'but I'll be covering for him tonight and …'

Praying Mantis hesitated, and instead of finishing his sentence, he suddenly fired off a series of brusque questions. Jerome angrily listened to the blunt queries, which began with: 'How do you feel?'

Jerome sarcastically muttered, 'Wonderful,' but his combative response did nothing to stem the flow of inquiries: 'Do you hear voices?' 'Do you have an appetite?' 'How are you sleeping?' A one-liner flashed through Jerome's mind, that a conclusion had to be the place you got to when you were tired of thinking, but he kept the rejoinder to himself.

Instead, he thought to himself that Dr. Praying Mantis had to specialise in taking histories from mute patients. At the same time, a shiver went through his body as he wondered what the hell was going on. This did not fit what had been described to him when he'd agreed to this project.

The last medical question, if it warranted that label, was thrown at him: 'What do you think is wrong with you?' Jerome began wondering if this strange creature was implying that there was nothing wrong with him. Without waiting for a response, Praying Mantis then hopped back out through the curtain, leaving Jerome feeling that this doctor had already decided on the diagnosis even before coming to see him. Had Praying Mantis read his file and seen the diagnosis listed? Certainly, at no stage did the doctor give any indication of being aware that Jerome was part of a trial experiment conducted by Klein and Anderson.

Jerome's tongue was dry, and he found it hard to talk. The nerves in his forehead tingled as if struggling to connect. The bitter thought hit him that he had fled England seeking a calmer, better, more fulfilling life; and here he was in a foreign country, stuck in a psychiatric ward as a patient, not having a clue as to what was going on.

Soon after, Carlos parted the curtain around the bed. As he approached, Jerome could see he was carrying a medication tray and immediately tensed up. Carlos asked him to lie on his stomach, which he did apprehensively, only to feel his pants being pulled down and a needle penetrating one buttock. It wasn't too painful, but it didn't take long for Jerome to begin feeling strange, as if enveloped by a cloud. He had difficulty focusing his eyes and found the thoughts in his head were tripping over each other, then hovering in the air like a bird with clipped wings. It was a weird sensation, one which scared him. Inertia started to ooze through his limbs like molasses, and though he fought against it, he had to give in to sleep. As he slipped into darkness, the thought entered his mind that he hadn't had time to change into his pyjamas.

○

Jerome struggled awake early the next morning, feeling completely wrung out and very groggy. Tom was still asleep, as were nearly all the others in the ward. The medication Carlos had given him couldn't have been a placebo!

For the rest of that day, Jerome fought against the anxiety that now fully enveloped, thinking his best bet was to follow Tom around, attending the program organised for that day. He attended activities, group therapy, occupational therapy, had some private time, but continued to feel detached, like a photo shot out of focus. The medication persisted in erasing some of his thinking and movements, and he knew this had to be what the real patients felt like all the time.

Jerome continually asked Tom to tell him who some of the other patients were, hoping this would distract and settle him. One man was called Horsey, because he used to own and train a lot of racehorses, including some very successful ones. He was also referred to as 'Nay'. Jerome was puzzled by this and then broke into a broad grin in spite of how he felt, when it hit him that the nickname was based on the sound horses make.

Tom explained that Horsey's wife had died suddenly many years ago, though he couldn't remember what illness she'd had. Horsey himself had then had a terrible fall whilst riding and was knocked out. As far as Tom could recall, Horsey had suffered quite a significant brain injury, bad enough that he could no longer devote himself to his business, which subsequently collapsed.

As Jerome began to learn a bit more about the other patients, he started seeing them more as human beings who had gone through traumas and had various needs as a result. He began visualising them as individuals, as opposed to the hotchpotch of humanity – if not non-humanity – he'd perceived on first entering the ward, something he was ashamed about now.

Jerome asked Tom about another patient, called Elliott, who had carrot-orange hair and repeatedly walked along an imaginary line that he obsessively had to follow. When Jerome wondered aloud what Elliott thought would happen if he didn't follow the line, Tom snapped, sounding irritated: 'I imagine it would be a lot worse than anything you could possibly think of. At least, that's how it would feel in his mind.'

Jerome replied, 'I think I know what you're saying. I walked with him yesterday and tried to avoid talking about things that might upset him. Occasionally I'd stop, and Elliot would manage to stop as well, and we just chatted for a little while.'

Tom didn't say anything, but his eyes posed the question, *What about?*

Jerome thought for a moment before responding: 'Well, I certainly didn't mention that imaginary line, because I understood how real it was to him. And I couldn't really talk to him about things in the outside world as he seemed divorced from that. So, I did my best to chat to him about things to do with himself, trying to hit on the happy parts, like good experiences from the past, or what was left of them.'

Jerome continued: 'Elliott told me how he used to be a keen fisherman. Would you believe, we spoke about flathead, sharks, what bait he preferred, and so on. As we talked, it was great seeing his face light up. I don't know what flicked the switch, turned the globe on. Maybe he could visualise himself pulling in a huge fish. Whatever it was, I thought to myself that too few people bother talking to him, or people like him. Possibly, they don't even see him as a human being, but rather as a diagnosis or a vegetable.'

Jerome quickly added, 'Apart from you.' He was worried that Tom might feel Jerome was putting him down, labelling him as amongst those who were insensitive to Elliott's needs. Then he pivoted back to Elliott: 'Sorry, I'm not feeling that well myself, so I shouldn't be playing the part of a psychiatrist. It's just that I wonder if the staff looking after him fail to see an image of him as a human being.'

Jerome left the conversation wondering if Tom believed that he was a trained doctor.

○

That afternoon, Jerome was dozing in the lounge, a communal area where patients could watch television or play board games. It was a place as drab and ugly as the other parts of the hospital. He was woken from his uneasy slumber by a cackle of laughter. Rubbing the sleep from his eyes, he heard Carlos tell another nursing aide that impotence was God's way of showing there were no hard feelings. There was a further loud cackle, in the wake of which Jerome thought to himself, rather bitterly, 'They're really tuned into their work.'

He immediately felt uncomfortable thinking that about Carlos, given that he was one of his more favoured staff members, possibly the only one. Carlos differed from the other staff because he was prepared to talk to the patients as if they were real people. He smiled and showed some warmth, though Jerome was not entirely sure how Carlos felt about his patients. What attracted Carlos to arm wrestle with Jerome? Was it a way of earning some pocket money or when he lost to Jerome, was it a way of buying freedom for his hand to slip downwards when they wrestled?

These thoughts prompted Jerome to once again reflect on how long he was going to be trapped in this situation.

One thing Jerome knew for certain was that he was determined to avoid shock treatment or being restrained, with ankle and wrists being strapped down. Tom confirmed this had happened to some of the other patients in the ward. Jerome knew it wouldn't happen to him with Klein or Anderson managing his case, but neither of them had shown up. There was now a large crack in his defences, through which his pent-up anxiety was starting to leak.

Getting to know the other patients better, learning more about the things that had created so much disruption in their lives and diminished their sense of wellbeing, was now one of the only things keeping him together. That and his friendship with Tom, of course. In addition to speaking with Elliott, he'd helped Andy drive 'the lions' away, and reassured Peter about the 'FBI plot', which sometimes morphed into the 'Zionist conspiracy', and sat enchanted watching Bobo send soapy rainbow balls floating to the ceiling. By doing this, he'd given them an outlet for their fears, whilst avoiding, as best he could, anything that might reinforce those fears. Sometimes he felt like he was starting to behave like a psychiatrist.

His growing familiarity with those around him, and his refusal to talk down to the distressed souls around him, meant the night sounds in his ward had ceased being anonymous noises of wretchedness or maniacal mirth. He'd even felt compelled to add his own voice to the heaving, raw cries of sexual desire that arose soon after the lights went out, as residents of the ward sought peace by pleasuring themselves.

The idea of joining in had felt weird, but then again, he thought, maybe he had more in common with his fellow patients than he felt comfortable acknowledging. So, he'd begun marching to the same rhythm, with no-one to judge him apart from himself. He masturbated to an exaggerated image of full lips, large breasts and the body that went with it, one that did not resemble any woman he had taken out in the past. He smelt the elusive fragrance as her hand moved downwards from his cheek and continued its path of exploration. His initial embarrassment and shame were soon submerged in the ecstasy of release.

Afterwards, he cleansed the bed and himself with sheets of toilet paper that he had salvaged. He knew that if he didn't clean up, no-one else would, and he would have to sleep in the excrement of his fantasy.

Wryly, he had told himself that if for any reason he needed to stop himself coming, all he had to do was to imagine that his sexual partner was Rote the Rottweiler.

Chapter 7

The following day, Jerome and Tom once again attended the mind-numbing activities of stuffing toys and finger painting. After the afternoon had been lost to these pastimes, they strolled outside, away from the others. Jerome turned to Tom and said, 'I know I've loaded you up with more detail and emotion than I would expect anyone to be able to handle in one go. However, I've started writing poetry, although I'm not sure poets consider it such.'

Jerome explained that he'd recently had a strong urge to document his life and the path that it had taken. But rather than keeping a regular diary, he had been completing poems, some of them started long ago, which he suspected gave a softer feel to some horrifying material that he was describing and writing about.

He laughed as he said about the poems being autobiographical. 'Any resemblance is purely coincidental. 'If you're interested, I can read you one that explains more about my past, in a much softer way.'

Tom smiled and nodded.

They sat themselves down on their bench. A big splinter it might be, but it felt like it was theirs. The sun was warm on their faces and there was no-one else around.

Jerome grinned. 'It just so happens that I'm carrying a copy of my poem. I've named it *Once I looked forward, now I reflect.*'

Nothing comes, it is arid land
Am I blocking pain from the past?
Or is it natural for memories not to last
as they drift and fade, could it be the beginning
of the word I am starting to dread,
with the brain fading and drifting
as it loses its memory and verve.
Once I looked forward, now I reflect.

Am I avoiding conflicts long gone,
maybe it's natural for memories not to last.
I fail to reassure myself, so the anxiety stays.
I often marvelled at my patient's recollection of dreams,
wondering if they were genuine or less than they seemed.
As a doctor I encouraged my patients to describe their dreams.
Once I looked forward, now I reflect.

I continued to be puzzled by the photographic recall
that some patients appeared to have,
were they bringing these treasures as gifts to please me?
or were they truly able to remember
revealing more than I could and can.
The first genuine memory that comes to my head
I'll start by telling you what I can't recall.
I have no personal memories of the hell that was the Holocaust.
Once I looked forward, now I reflect.

I can't remember being arrested when thirteen days old.
I can't recall the labour camp imprisoning my parents
all this I learned from Washington records
where the events and my crime were described.
The paperwork there revealed my misdemeanour
was my mother being Jewish, which she passed on to me.
Maybe it's a blessing my memory can't recall
The horrors back then.
Once I looked forward, now I reflect.

After nine months submerged in this horror,
we were helped to escape
assisted by a Polish policeman
who I know not by name.
It continues to puzzle me how a child survives
in a man-made hell not aimed at supporting life.
A month after, we were helped to escape.
The camp was destroyed, in the true meaning of the word,
wiping itself clean of prisoners and all.
Once I looked forward, now I reflect.

Some were killed immediately,
others were sent to be gassed
their deaths heralded by billowing smoke
contaminating the sky and those that stood by.
Once I looked forward, now I reflect.

The killing machine aimed to ensure
that no progeny remained
to taint the earth as before.
This from records revealed to me
As I have no memory of it
But the graphic images described in print
go festering in my brain
Memory's place has been taken

by images constructed
from what I've read and learned
of other peoples' suffering.
Yes, we escaped the camp
but retained the hell.
Once I looked forward, now I reflect.

We hid amongst strangers in Warsaw
but not as ourselves.
Some neighbours suspected yet remained silent
showing courage that deserves to be admired.
I wasn't told that I was Jewish, as children can blab
so, I ran with the mob hurling the same abuse
unknowingly directing it
at my Jewish sisters and brothers,
not realising they were me.
Once I looked forward, now I reflect.

We fled the killing fields of Poland
as the Russians moved in
we were seeking sanctuary
where we could live and be free.
Once I looked forward, now I reflect.

We sailed to England, sleeping on deck
overwhelmed by the odour of rotting fish below.
We were traumatised but free, far from the Europe we knew.
Lots of questions remain that puzzle me
such as why was I circumcised
showing a Jew – it was me
so why would my parents label me
with death so close.
Fortunately, they had the sense to arrange
a Jewish doctor, to reverse the process and hide me.
Once I looked forward, now I reflect.

My parents and I emerged damaged somehow
in the UK I struggled, feeling different
the way I dressed and looked, the food I ate
my parents with accents, not yet able to debate.
Hearing cries of bloody Jew, kike go home
greeted me in places that
I was not allowed to call home
Once I looked forward, now I reflect.

I forced myself to go to school
but differences remained and snowballed
gathering speed and continuing to cause pain.
But I continue to wonder
whether having memories
is so wonderful and great.
Maybe it depends on whether they are memories
That one can gleefully celebrate, rather than hate.
Once I looked forward, now I reflect.

As I grew older and more at ease
I began to feel urges
such as the thrust in my loins
now I have scattered memories
and images of love and lust
as I recall myself lacking
the courage to act and call.
Once I looked forward, now I reflect.

Thankfully the memories became warmer
and softer by far
As I met someone I cared for dearly,
yet didn't have the courage to let her know,
scared whether the future would be hard or soft
eventually parting, trying to leave the past behind.
Once I looked forward, now I reflect.

I can recall the fragrance of flowers, the dew on the grass
the pleasure experienced gazing out
in the early morning light.
Some of what was lacking in life
was retrieved walking with friends
and together inhaling the night air scent.
These are memories I cling to, as they soften
some of the pain and hurt of despair.
Once I looked forward, now I reflect.

My confidence took a battering
in those early years.
making it hard to value the person that I was
and continued to aspire to be.
There were parts of me I wanted to hide
as I came from a family others could not abide
As I age, I hope my understanding improves
both of myself and those around me too.
Once I looked forward, now I reflect.

As I age, I want people to know and see me
for the person I am and want to be
not judging me by the family I come from
who they can't respect nor accept
wanting them not to be blinded, but to view me as myself.
Once I looked forward, now I reflect.

I worry whether they can truly see me
I wish there wasn't always a part
that had to remain hidden, that their eyes couldn't see
I aspire to be as open as I possibly can
hoping people can relate to me as an honest man
Once I looked forward, now I reflect.

I've come to a new country
wishing to start afresh
where people can judge me on what they see
free of contamination in the perceptions they hold.
By not typecasting me,
they are left free to decide,
finding my qualities are what they like
rather than being the product of a family they despise.
Once I looked forward, now I reflect.

I look forward to studying
and becoming a psychiatrist for life
I want to be honest and not live a lie
to be able to be open and trusting and not on guard
Removing the burden of constantly measuring it all.
Eventually free and able to look forward again.
Once I looked forward, now I reflect.

I find I get down at times when I look
at humanity and where it is heading.
I am starting to see that all of us
are lacking in various degrees,
leaving us prejudiced and hurtful at times,
but being aware and trying to deal with it,
that is what counts, even without rhyme.
Once I looked forward, now I reflect.

I've noted how evil occurs
when good people stand by doing nothing
creating the green light and confidence
for evil to feel nourished and spring forth.
Sadly, evil appears unavoidable in our world
with so many capable of hating,
even the newborn
and on occasion even you and me.
Once I looked forward, now I reflect.

I guess I am starting to look to the future
still pondering whether we can all be evil at times
no-one can say for sure that their thoughts or behaviour
are always pure and sublime.
I feel we are all capable of hurting
both strangers and friends alike
at times attempting to quell the rage as best we can
and trying to be honest with ourselves and them.
Once I looked forward, now I reflect.

Possibly circumstances in life and surroundings
may determine whether we move towards love or hate
as I get older, should I be assessing,
the meaning of my life, examining the time that's been
or the time remaining,
wondering if I need to measure at all?
Once I looked forward, now I reflect.

I am starting to believe it's preferable just to live
where the meaning of life is what I make it to be
and having the courage to stand for the things I find important.
I don't need religion to explain the purpose of life
as I believe religion should be treating people
the way we want to be treated ourselves.
Once I looked forward, now I reflect.

The quality of life depends on
people that we love and trust,
this is what gives meaning to life,
whilst trying to avoid getting bogged down
in things I can't possibly change,
but not remaining silent when others are suffering
the pain of prejudice all day and night
Once I looked forward, now I reflect.

Hopefully I have learnt
when to be silent and when to speak up
looking out for me and thee.
I want my life to have less hurdles and traps
some of which I may be responsible for
I want to be less angry and resentful of the past
as people hopefully begin seeing me
for the person I am.
Once I looked forward, now I reflect.

I want to be at peace with myself
hoping one day to share my love
to have a structure that gives meaning to life.
Once I looked forward, now I reflect.

In the years to come, as I get older
my memory and recall are likely to diminish
I believe that's why I obsessively cling to photos,
hoping they remind me of the past
as I have lost so many memories where no photos or gravestones exist
unable to remind me or pay homage to those who are missing.
Needing memories and reminders
which can be links that remain, long after I cease to last.
Once I looked forward, now I reflect.

I am coming to terms with the knowledge
that there are many things I can't control
yet it will be soothing to know
that I have lived life meaningfully and openly
buoyed by the warmth of those close by my side
accompanying me on the journey of life.
Once I looked forward, now I reflect.

'OK Tom,' said Jerome, 'I expect you to memorise this poem within say three days. How does that sound?'

Jerome's grin put his comment in perspective.

Tom just smiled benignly, not bothering to speak.

Jerome then recited a much shorter verse called *Evil*, touching on evil and the impact it can have in the lives of all.

What is evil you may well ask?
To define and predict it becomes quite a task.
I ponder often whether evil is so widespread,
yet I know deep down that it's present, not only in my head
Whether it be on land or sea and even lying in bed
so in varying degrees, we can all be led.
None of us can be sure
that we are totally free
of the underlying rage and urges
life experiences can decree and mould
that can readily harm both you and me.
Life experiences have the potential to make us grow or sink,
and as I age I begin myself to tell
that evil is what evil does.
It corrupts and hurts the perpetrator and spectator alike,
who can both end up engulfed in a personal hell.
Some of my friends are ailing or dead
and some survive.
Was it the roll of the dice or someone's brilliant head?
With all these incidents from the past,
when we congregate, we relive
experiences from now and before
noting how they are conducted
by those who care and are still alive,
some left with concern and anxiety filling their head,
others wondering what to measure and see,
believing strongly the need to record,

hoping it will connect them with the past and present, and even
with the future yet to see
some will emerge with considerably more knowledge
than ever before.
But I am still wondering what it all means.
Is it preferable to live and be
though wondering how we best measure the value of the life that
we live and see?

As he fell silent, it struck Jerome that he often was aware and preoccupied with the evils of the world, but at the same time his own behaviour could benefit from a scrub.

To be genuine, he needed to stay aware of the things he did which hurt others. He realised that in his mind, if women had sex with him, or with anyone probably, he would tend to view them as somewhat cheapened. He'd struggled with that attitude for most of his life. Having had his fill, he often abruptly terminated seeing them, and moved on to the next challenge. He felt, if he was being honest with himself, that the way he related to women was collecting conquests essentially for his own sexual gratification before moving on to the next conquest.

He recalled a young Asian woman, a call girl, and blushed to himself as he remembered deriving pleasure from her passivity, her dilating eyes expressing her fear as he entered her.

So, when the world is cleansed, he realised, he should be part of that queue.

Chapter 8

It was the end of another day at Riverdale, and Jerome found himself obsessing more and more as to what might have gone wrong to prevent Dr. Klein and Dr. Anderson coming to see him as prearranged. He felt the moisture of fear accumulating and shuddered at the thought that he might be trapped with no way out. Surely someone must know if anything had gone wrong or when the doctors were likely to come. Now he could only fantasise about what might be going on, eventually creating a vacuum of ideas.

Jerome kept attempting to ask staff when his doctors would come and see him, but the staff stood there sullen and mute. He felt the responses were all useless at best and somewhat hostile, causing him to feel increasingly fearful, irritable, and worried. Some staff just stood and glared at him when he asked about the whereabouts of his treating doctors, and none of them offered to find out and get back to him. With the lack of explanation, Jerome became increasingly frustrated, unsure if they knew and weren't telling him. He thought he might get a better response from Carlos as Carlos didn't glare or walk off. It was not a blessing however as the net result was still an absence of any information. Carlos just grinned and changed the topic with a query about the time of their next scheduled arm-wrestle.

In attempting to escape his mass of thoughts and escalating fear, Jerome took himself out onto the hospital grounds, only to find the fear came with him. As he wove between mature trees and poorly tended flower beds, Jerome again found himself contemplating Jill, who'd been dominating his thoughts more and more lately.

Jill was a woman he had developed a close bond with when he was living in Birmingham. But while he'd loved the warmth and intimacy of her friendship, underneath that was the constant fear that he wasn't quite ready for a lasting relationship. Deeper down was the fear of yet another rejection.

Jerome was aware that he rarely initiated a friendship but rather would wait for the other person to indicate that they wanted one. He did this to diminish the possibility of being knocked back, but even so, fear of the pain of rejection would take over. He came to feel that the pain of not having a close relationship was less than the hurt of developing a close bond and losing it down the track.

As he walked the grounds without aiming for any specific end point, the thoughts about Jill became confrontational head on without any significant warning. Not for the first time he questioned himself as to whether he felt guilty about the way he'd ultimately cast Jill aside.

Jill herself had significant issues, having been born out of wedlock, and living with her mother, who struggled financially without family support. Her father had fled the family many years earlier and she'd had no contact with him since then. Over the years there had been a string of men who had come to visit her mother, many of whom appeared undesirable to Jill. She tried to keep a distance from them, but this didn't prevent them from trying to flirt with her. Jerome found himself wondering, not for the first time, whether there was any such thing as a stable, honest, open family life, or if people just pretended there was.

The fact that Jill was non-Jewish did not bother Jerome. However, it had been an issue in the past with his father and then his stepfather, both of whom had objected to him going out with non-Jewish girls. Jerome had been amazed at this prejudice, considering the men giving voice to it had suffered so much themselves from the prejudice of other people.

Jerome found Jill to be clever, pretty, and perhaps best of all, she appeared to like him for himself, not judging him by the family he came from. They avoided consummating their relationship, but they did indulge in heavy petting, and Jerome felt their closeness was intimate and warm. In a way, Jerome saw himself and Jill as being two lost souls.

What had drawn him to Jill initially was the safety of her trying to win his approval. It was clear from her behaviour that she liked him and wanted to get closer to him. Jerome had then felt free to assess her as being attractive or not. She had a lovely face, a firm figure, and a prominent bosom, all of which appealed to him. He avoided thinking too far ahead, about whether she could be a long-term partner.

Jerome felt uncomfortable with the idea of having sex with a woman he respected, if the woman was not yet married. Over the years, he'd fantasised having sex with a range of imaginary partners, and occasionally had found relief in a local brothel, though this always left him feeling sullied and guilty, disturbed by the thought that he might be exploiting the young women involved, and knowing that he was. He could not escape the feeling that sex should be reserved for a partner one was married to, although that held the possibility that the woman would merely fulfil her marital obligations rather than admitting to having any sensual needs herself.

When Jerome decided that he would leave Birmingham and start afresh by studying psychiatry in another country, he side-stepped confiding in Jill about his plans. He had no doubt that it would hurt her quite a deal when it happened. Eventually, when he told her he would be leaving in a few weeks' time, he avoided her gaze, knowing that it meant a complete break in their relationship. She was not going to be part of his new life. He knew it and so did she.

Even though he was determined to act in this way, he was aware of feeling some shame about it. But he could not afford to carry with him any part of the burden that had weighed on his past life. He wanted to begin his adult life again, surrounded by people who didn't know him or his family or his past. It was akin to a surgeon who could only work in a sterile setting.

Tears pricked at Jerome's eyes as he recalled the two of them sitting in a park in the pre-dawn gloom, cuddling and waiting for the sun's light to begin glistening on the cut grass. Since childhood Jerome found peace on his own gazing at the early morning light, and it meant even more when he was able to share it with someone he cared about.

He had forceful rationalisations for his behaviour, centred on how his self-renewal had to involve being with people not prejudiced about him like before, but his conscience did not totally believe him. The mature way Jill had handled her sadness made it difficult for him to cast aside the guilt that he knew was rightly his to own. The more decently she behaved in response to her pending loss, the harder it became to shift blame from himself. She had shared tears of separation but avoided the words of recrimination which were rightly hers to utter. He held her tightly then discarded.

O

The routine of the day in the psychiatric ward had dragged on, and Jerome imagined that for the real patients, most days were like this, with little variation. Then, as the clock ticked around to 6 pm, he did as he had done every evening prior to seeing Praying Mantis' narrow face: he sat on his bed, anxiously hoping that it would be Dr. Klein or Dr. Anderson's turn to appear through the curtains drawn around him.

When the curtain that he had drawn around his bed bulged, Jerome thought his hopes were about to be realised. But he was horrified to see that he was again being visited by Praying Mantis, whose real name, he'd discovered, was Dr Mangis. To make matters worse, the doctor was accompanied by Sister Rote, and they both wore what Jerome felt were unusual expressions on their faces, looks that he could not decipher. That thought quickly receded as Dr Mangis began talking, his words even more rapid than last visit.

'Jerome, I'll be your doctor for the time being,' said Dr Mangis. 'There's been a terribly tragic accident. A short while ago, we received definite confirmation that a small plane carrying Dr. Klein and Dr and Mrs. Anderson on a trip into the countryside, crashed, killing everyone on board. They all died immediately, apparently, but that's small consolation to their loved ones and friends.'

Dr Mangis wiped his eyes with the back of one hand, while Sister Rote remained unusually quiet. Jerome's thoughts ricocheted in all directions, like the steel balls in a pinball cabinet.

Jerome attempted to reassure himself that if he just confessed to the staff that he was a young doctor who had come to Riverdale for psychiatric training, and that he wasn't really a patient, that would sort things out. Sure, he would feel like a goose, but it was the key to exiting this nightmare situation. Then he experienced a further flare of anxiety as he recalled Klein and Anderson emphasising that no-one apart from themselves and Jerome knew about the trial they were setting up in the ward.

The mathematics were basic enough, so basic that they began to engulf him. Events had led to a nightmare where of the three who knew what was going on, only he remained. And he was troubled, terribly troubled, by the fact that the staff had not picked up on him not really being a patient. But he still couldn't imagine that once he explained everything to them, they wouldn't believe him.

Jerome knew he should probably be feeling something about the deaths of the people on board the plane, but it was hard to focus on that while the concern about getting out of the hospital was unresolved. As his concerns and thoughts continued to fly in all directions, he began worrying about whether the deaths of these two doctors would affect the training program he was in.

Jerome struggled to control his anxiety. He didn't feel there was anyone he could share his fears with. With great difficulty, in a stuttering voice, he attempted to explain to Dr Mangis just who he was and why he was there.

But what began as a measured explanation quickly became a barrage of words that exploded from his mouth. Dr Mangis started edging backwards, simultaneously calling out to a nursing aide, asking her to bring something to help Jerome settle down; Sister Rote had already vanished through the curtains.

Overwhelmed by confusion, Jerome could only hear fragments of what Dr Mangis was saying: 'Thinks he's a doctor … garbled story that I couldn't … a conspiracy with Klein and Anderson … guinea pig for some experiment … somewhat psychotic, really delusional … could become aggressive … antipsychotics for injection …'

The curtains parted and Jerome saw Sister Rote speedily approaching, carrying a medication tray and a paper cup. Dr Mangis attempted to reassure him, saying, 'Relax Jerome. This is the same medication that Dr. Klein …' The stream of words was abruptly cut as Jerome's right hand shot out, sending the tray and cup flying. As the psychiatrist and the matron fled the room, Jerome kept yelling: 'I'm really a doctor! I am! I'm a doctor!!'

The muscular form of Carlos entered the room. Dr. Mangis hesitantly informed Jerome that Carlos would restrain him, just to be safe, while the doctor gave him an injection. He tried to reassure Jerome that he would feel a lot calmer in a half-hour or so.

All the while, Jerome kept shouting, 'I'm a doctor! Why can't you see that?!'

Carlos chuckled as he said, 'Yeah, and I'm Jesus Christ.' He then called out to a male nurse standing nearby. 'Hey Mac, Jerome says that he's a doctor. Do you wanna ask him some medical questions?'

'Yep,' Mac snorted. 'Ask him if he wants the needle in his right butt or his left one?'

As Dr Mangis readied the injection, he told the aides to cut it out and stop making fun of Jerome. Then Carlos and Mac held down Jerome as the medication was plunged into his bloodstream.

Soon Jerome felt a wave of drowsiness take possession of his body, his muscles weakening, his eyes losing the struggle to focus.

He slept till four in the morning, then woke with his body lathered in sweat. He discovered that he was even less free now than he'd been on hearing that Klein and Anderson were dead – straps restrained his limbs and prevented him from leaving the bed.

It was just after daybreak that Tom crept over to him, whispering. 'You need to cool it buddy, otherwise they'll keep treating you like this, maybe even give you that good old shock treatment.'

Jerome wasn't sure if Tom believed that he was a doctor, but he was certain that Tom's advice was sound. He knew that unless he changed his behaviour, they would continue restraining and injecting him, and maybe give him ECT.

As he lay there bound tightly to the bed frame, Tom having gone quietly back to his own bed, Jerome found his mind submerged by a flood of thoughts. For years he had wondered how an individual decided who and what they were. Did they base it on what people told them, and risk feeling worthless, or on what they told themselves? Did they base it on personal success, or did they somehow develop a sense of intrinsic worth?

Other thoughts began weighing heavily on him, in particular, generalising from his own experience, about the impure stains that humanity was leaving around the world. He felt crushed by the possibility that all of humanity was capable of doing evil. He tried to soften this blow by thinking of righteous individuals who showed caring and kindness even in the face of personal risk and danger. But was it possible even they could commit evil in certain circumstances?

Tom had once smilingly suggested that maybe some people, like Jerome and himself, had to live in some degree of hell when they were alive, to make up for missing out on it later when they died.

O

In the days that followed, Jerome was submerged in anger, anxiety and occasionally despair. The faint hope persisted in him that someone else had been privy to the research trial Klein and Anderson had set up, but the possibility of this was diminished in his mind by knowledge of how the two doctors had been focused – extremely so – on keeping the experiment under wraps.

For some reason, it made him remember what an American astronaut once described about a journey he had made to the moon. During the space flight, the astronaut couldn't help thinking that the spaceship he was in had been assembled from parts supplied by a firm that likely had offered the cheapest tender. For Jerome, this reflected the fact that even the most professional plan could have a weak spot.

Unable to convince anyone he didn't belong in the psychiatric ward, Jerome increasingly began to feel that bad things and evil could occur equally by design or by chance. For years he had been identified as the son of 'those alcoholic bums', and now he had acquired the label of a chronic, severely disturbed psychiatric patient. The problem was, he knew that, unlike Tom, staying in this cage was not an option he could ever consider.

This whole nightmare had started with the word *yes*. The *yes,* he'd said to the research project. He felt he might regret using that word for the remainder of his life, however long that turned out to be.

Yet again, Jerome felt anger, resentment, and self-pity well up inside him, and he did his best to push the feelings back down.

From time to time over the years, Jerome had taken stock of his life, and on doing so felt that it had consisted of one hurdle after another which he'd had to clear in order to survive. And survive he had, but at what cost? He could not tolerate the thought of his life continuing in the same pattern in the future.

Jerome yet again couldn't avoid contemplating how much better Tom was at handling the stress in his life compared to Jerome. He also noted how Tom appeared to carry much less anger and resentment around with him.

Over the next few days, Jerome was freed from the restraints, but they were often reapplied with little to no warning. There seemed to be no rhyme or reason governing when this was done. By and by, Jerome came to understand that if he became agitated, or complained that the staff weren't listening to him or didn't believe his story about being a doctor, it was more likely the restraints would be used; only being removed once he'd received his injection to settle him down.

If this was meant to be therapy, it didn't feel that way to Jerome. It felt more like being kept under control.

Still, Jerome found that he could be more settled if he tried to do so, and this was when he made an effort to interact with the other patients in the ward. He was seeing them in a clearer way as individual human beings now, with a variety of personalities and problems. It also helped him feel less isolated, as he was more part of a group.

Sure, there was Tom, but having access to other ward patients leant a further measure of support, he felt. Some of them were able to share their own fears or dreams, whereas it struck Jerome that outside of the hospital, people tended to hide such things, loathe to drop their defences, keeping the bulk of their emotions hidden from sight. In the ward, a lot of this armour had been shelved. Jerome guessed that much of this was involuntary, but regardless, shelved it was. He pondered which was the healthier approach, whether the defences people adopted outside the ward were necessarily of benefit to them. He chuckled at the idea that in some ways, there was a basic honesty about aspects of severe mental illness and madness, because it wasn't hidden.

Was it possible that one group could learn from the other as to which features were healthier in the long run? Could one let too much out or bottle up too much? He was certain that some degree of control of one's emotions was important, but he was equally certain that excessive control could be damaging. He was sure that the ability to share emotions with others was an essential part of healthy relationships, while at the same time he knew this was something he had feared doing over most of his life.

He had long carried secrets with him, things he felt shouldn't be divulged. And this habit created obstacles to what he desired most of all, or at least what he told himself he most desired: the ability to form an intimate, trusting relationship. One that survived long term, and nurtured a warm, trusting family life; a family life dramatically different to the one in which he grew up.

Chapter 9

Day Fifteen

Jerome had been in the ward for just over two weeks and had avoided being restrained or more heavily sedated. Interacting with Tom and to a lesser degree some of the other patients helped, but it was fragile and just keeping the anxiety and fear at bay.

Then a few days down the track, Dr Mangis informed him that he planned to present Jerome's case to a group of psychiatrists and psychologists at a clinical meeting.

'Don't worry about it,' said Dr Mangis. 'Some of the top brains in mental health will be there, and we'll have the benefit of their combined wisdom and experience.'

Jerome suppressed what he really wanted to say: *If they're like you, it will be the blind leading the blind.*

Dr Mangis went on to explain how he hoped that, after Jerome's clinical features had been presented, the collective wisdom of the assembled therapists would help Mangis formulate a plan that would speed up Jerome's recovery.

It was soon apparent to Jerome that he was not being asked for permission, merely being informed about what would happen – as a courtesy, so to speak.

When the day of the conference arrived, Jerome found himself seated at the front of a cavernous meeting room, which had the same bland look and lack of decoration that distinguished the rest of the facility, while what seemed to be a myriad of voices discussing him as if he was not present. It reminded him in a bizarre way of dining out with a group of friends at a restaurant and talking without inhibition, as if the waiters serving the group were somehow deaf and could not hear their conversation.

A memory came to him of eating out at a grand restaurant with some friends. He'd pontificated about sexual desire, specifically the fact that fear did not necessarily diminish that desire. He remembered talking to the buxom young lady sitting next to him, after both he and she had been well lubricated with a good red. Immediately after he'd informed her that one could be sexually aroused even in a state of intense fear, a waiter crept up and in a highly theatrical manner yelled 'BOOO!' into his dining companion's ear. He doubted that his new friend had been sexually aroused at that point, but it prompted marked hilarity and helped him break the ice in getting to know someone he had barely known before.

Recalling this incident helped Jerome deal with the discomfort of having a group of professionals talk about him as if he was invisible. Words and phrases floated up to him like "paranoid", "delusions of professionalism", "thought his file had been falsified". Jerome thought to himself bitterly, 'how can you not have delusions of professionalism when you have dozens of professionals talking about you?'

He heard Dr Mangis tell the assembled group that Jerome appeared to have no extended family support and a very sparse past history.

'The reason for a sparse past history should be bloody obvious,' Jerome thought to himself.

If you did not talk to the patient and listen to their responses, how could their history be anything, but sparse? He wondered what being talked about in this manner could do to the level of one's sexual arousal and decided it could only be a downer.

Dr Mangis then told the audience that Sister Rote felt Jerome had psychopathic qualities, and she had been pushing for Dr Mangis to treat him with shock treatment. Dr Mangis said he totally disagreed with the matron's assessment, believing instead that Jerome's diagnosis was more akin to a transient psychosis. The doctor asserted that this disorder caused Jerome to be out of touch with reality at times, and to be fragile emotionally. He suspected that drug use in the past had played a role in the illness.

Jerome tried to detach himself from what was being said by thinking of happier times. However, he found it extremely difficult to recall those times, and strongly doubted they could match what he was experiencing now or had experienced over recent years. He attempted to reassure himself that this nightmare was exactly that, and once he woke up, it would be gone. The staff would eventually come to their senses, and he would be surrounded by their ashamed faces. He tried to hang on to the image of apologies flowing from their lips.

When the meeting was finally over and he was being escorted back to his ward, Jerome promised himself that he would carry on playing the role of a good patient until the truth came out, giving himself a pep talk about what he needed to do. It was the only way to deal with his fears.

The fear that if things continued in the present way it would wear him down, just as so many of the other poor souls in the ward had been worn down; his energy and drive severely depleted. The fear that he had little capacity for getting out of the hospital and going on to live a happy, stable life – away from the medication, the anxiety and early depressive symptoms, sapped his ability to function.

Then there was the fear that the misdiagnosis by the staff currently treating him would become a self-fulfilling prophesy.

Jerome had realised that if he was to maintain his sanity, he needed to focus on the outside world – which for him at present was the ward he was imprisoned in.

O

Jerome's interactions with the other patients improved markedly, although none could match the closeness he felt with Tom. He set himself the task of learning more of their names and allowing them to speak to him about concerns they might have.

To varying degrees, they began sharing their anxieties, which made the night terror sounds they emitted less anonymous, and he was able to see what underlay the sounds of wretchedness and maniacal mirth. He became more familiar with the jungle animals and spiders that supposedly stalked these men, and the conspiracies that allegedly threatened to harm them. He continued to be fascinated by Bobo's soapy coloured bubbles and the drifting mass of colour they created. He encouraged the men to talk about their happiness as well as their distress, by asking questions to do with their personal lives, hobbies and other activities.

As well as distracting Jerome from his own problems, he believed or maybe just hoped, that what he was doing was also beneficial to the others. He wryly smiled to himself that he was functioning as a psychiatrist, but mainly to help himself at this point.

Whatever the cause, he found that within a week Dr Mangis had stopped giving him injections, although the doctor was now treating Jerome with tablets that were major tranquilisers for his alleged psychosis. Unfortunately, Jerome could not avoid swallowing the tablets, as the staff were always on the lookout for that kind of deception.

Jerome even enjoyed the company of Carlos, having forgiven him for mocking his claim that he was a doctor. The men played backgammon and continued to arm wrestle for small amounts of money. That said, Jerome remained uncertain and cautious about Carlos' feelings towards him. It was still the case that during the arm wrestling, Carlos' hand would sometimes 'slip' and end up in the vicinity of Jerome's groin, creating considerable discomfort. So far, Jerome had dealt with it by pushing Carlos vigorously in the chest, as if that was part of the competition.

Tom had recently cautioned Jerome to keep a watch on what he said and discussed with Carlos. Tom said there had been some talk recently that Carlos had connections with a sect. Tom didn't know the name of the sect, but had heard they were antipsychiatry. He said he knew nothing more, but felt that someone connected with a sect that was antipsychiatry – well, you've had to wonder why he'd be working here, and felt Jerome needed to be wary of any conversations he had with Carlos.

There were occasions when Jerome couldn't keep the anxiety at a level he could cope with, and it would build up to an episode of outright panic. Seeing Ewan coming back from shock treatment one morning unsettled Jerome. As Ewan walked down a corridor, he clenched his right hand into a fist, and the fist then became an iron hammer that slammed into the wall, splintering the plaster, and creating a snowstorm of small fibres. Ewan mostly seemed to be a gentle soul, and Jerome couldn't help but wonder if the ECT was causing him to be manic and aggressive.

Jerome also learnt that some in the ward had been inpatients for close to seven years. It terrified him to think that he might be trapped there for such an enormous amount of time. He just couldn't believe that no-one was able to discern that he wasn't ill and did not need to be there. It had now been over two weeks since his admission, and it was getting harder and harder to believe things would come right.

These intense worries made him feel lightheaded and confused. He was experiencing frequent headaches and bouts of sweating. His body and mind found it difficult to slow down or to be at rest. His thoughts became more fragmented, and he noted an escalating preoccupation with issues of evil and disasters. He began fearing that he would sink into a quagmire of doubt, with his life stumbling from one catastrophe to another.

He felt impelled to jot down a poem that expressed his feelings on evil and sin.

I can no longer hide and blame
the people who preached
telling me we were not all the same.
Yes, they preached their gospel of unrelenting hate
but it was I who gave them entry through the gate.
I could have learnt from those that cared,
nurturing the love, respect and capacity to be fair.
Yet somehow, I let the evil seep in
creating the garbage I now recognise as sin.
I sought out differences that I could hate
then stood idly by whilst others
met up with their fate.
So, I've soiled that blank canvas there from the start,
leaving me wondering if it's too late to cleanse my slate.
Is it too late to undo this hate?

Do I blame others or start with me?

Jerome felt like he had struggled for a major part of his life underneath dark clouds and in the deep shadows of tall mountains, and though he had eventually broken through the clouds and climbed those mountains, he could not accept that the rest of his life would involve continually overcoming such challenges. This was the realisation that tormented him when he woke up one morning and lay in bed, his body motionless but his mind speeding across vast wastelands of worry. He wished he had just slept for longer and didn't have to put up with these feelings. But he couldn't escape them.

He wondered if he should just give up the idea of escaping and accept living in the hospital as a way of hiding from the traumas of his past, just as Tom had. For one thing, he had no idea how he could manage to escape from the ward and live on the outside. It had to be done in a way that ensured he would not be recaptured and brought back to Riverdale. He certainly couldn't rely on being discharged, as there was still no evidence that this had been the experience of any of the patients in the ward.

Suddenly, Jerome felt a deep pang of guilt at the idea of escape, as if part of him believed he deserved to be locked up in the ward. Before he could stop himself, he began mentally listing all the people he felt he had let down in the past, followed by a tide of self-recriminations and ruminations. He thought back to his mother's death by suicide after he'd left home and found he could not avoid some degree of self-blame. Deep down, he knew that, in some way, he had contributed to her death.

And then there was Jill. He knew before he broke off the relationship how hurtful it would be for her. But he still went ahead and did it, telling himself Jill was just an inevitable and necessary casualty, deceiving himself with the idea that his only course of action had been to escape from Birmingham. Now, he was contemplating leaving behind another person he cared for: Tom.

Sure, doing all of this possibly shielded him from the hurt he would have experienced when important people in his life left him. But in reality, he was doing the very same thing, all the while depriving himself and others of relationships that were treasured.

Chapter 10

As the days at Riverdale wore on, Jerome's mind kept returning to several themes. He repeatedly asked himself if the fantasy that he had at times of staying in one place and living alongside people he cared about could ever happen in real life. It would mean risking those people leaving him, but he believed what he was doing now, the isolation he was imposing on himself, was equally painful and destructive. He was starting to face the reality that his habit of breaking away from people had done little to encourage a sense of happiness in his life, and that sticking with the relationships stood a better chance of promoting wellbeing.

He also kept visualising the boarding house that was to be his abode when he properly commenced his psychiatric training. It was a charming old wooden building set in expansive grounds centred on a luscious expanse of green lawn, with woods nearby. He recalled the sounds and sights of a variety of birds which would be his neighbours, and how he'd been reassured by Mrs Sykes' orderly approach, where everything had a name and a place. What would she be thinking now, after weeks had elapsed since she'd last heard from him? Would she be wondering what had happened to her new boarder?

He fantasised about and yearned for a life with a meaningful partner, with whom he possibly would have children, creating a warm family setting. He realised the irony of his wish for this pattern of behaviour, as for most of his earlier life he had feared rejection and prevented himself from getting too close to anyone for too long. The saying came to mind again: *Physician, heal thyself.*

All the while, he found himself searching for a way to escape from the hospital, even though it meant leaving Tom behind. He continued to feel that getting away from Riverdale was the priority. The other things he desired continued to remain in the too-hard basket.

Jerome thought about Jill yet again, missing her, and the warm, trusting intimacy of their relationship, where it had been apparent she wanted him as a partner. This was closely followed by a pang of shame at the abrupt way he had terminated the relationship. His rationale had been the desire to start life afresh without people who knew him, but his conscience did not totally believe him – not now, nor back then. Why he couldn't have begun that process with Jill was something he'd yet to examine.

Would there ever be a time when he could stay out in the open and not need to hide or cover himself up?

His thoughts were becoming far too negative again. Seemingly out of nowhere, he started thinking about how people who visited abattoirs were probably more likely to give up eating meat and become vegetarians, or so he had read. Would the same thing happen, he wondered, if people visited Holocaust memorials and former concentration camps? Could that diminish the risk of them acting in a cruel or vicious way themselves? He doubted that outcome. Again, his thoughts gravitated to a comparison of animal and human behaviour that he had once read, and he realised he still tended to believe the observation that animals acted on instinct and need and were fundamentally less cruel than humans. If a dog attacked, it would most likely be for food or self-defence, not for sadistic pleasure.

Jerome knew that whilst it was valid to examine all these ideas and feelings, in a way it led to him living his life in his head. Could it be time to take the plunge and confront what he was avoiding through his intellectualisations? Could it be as simple as living life rather than just thinking about it?

Maybe it was time to be honest with himself and act on the awareness that, yes, close relationships could cause pain, but he should stick with them and deal with the emotions that followed. After all, a close relationship itself wasn't the major problem, rather it was the anticipated pain of things not working out, which fuelled his destructive habit of avoidance, running, escaping the possibility of proximity.

Having once again retreated into his thoughts, Jerome grimaced, wondering if he would ever find someone to share his contemplations seeing as he mainly spoke to himself.

His mind circled back to the Holocaust, to how it only happened because most of the world stood by and did nothing. A German academic who specialised in studies of the Holocaust, and World War 2 more generally, had told him that only two countries had acted decently during the war: Albania and Bulgaria. Denmark had enjoyed a reputation for helpfulness, but apparently this had not occurred to the degree that people tended to believe. The thought then struck Jerome that perhaps he was using the Holocaust experience as a rationale for not getting close to people.

Yes, it was valid to try and understand human behaviour, man's propensity for being cruel. But he was determined to separate that process from the steps he needed to take to live life fully, by allowing some people in to share that life with him.

His thoughts took an even more negative path as he pondered his realisation that if Pearl Harbor had not occurred, he probably would not be alive now, as America had appeared to have no wish to enter the war until it was forced to do so. It had troubled him when he read that America in fact had performed racial profiling even before Germany, not being keen on welcoming Chinese or Jewish migrants into the country, although that stand had altered in more recent times. He told himself yet again that it was time to stop talking life in his head and rather begin living it, warts and all.

At moments like these, it seemed to Jerome that he was dragging himself through the mud of the past and floundering in it, rather than resolving anything. He thought again about how, in Birmingham, he had resorted to prostitutes and had felt guilty, soiled. He'd felt particularly bad at what the experience could be doing to those women – the young, the very young, and simultaneously aged beyond their years. Would sex achieve a measure of respectability in marriage, he wondered? God, life could be so confusing.

Part of the problem was believing that women had a range of sexual desires and there was nothing deviant or cheap about them feeling that way. Logic might be telling him that, but he was far from comfortable with embracing the idea, and certainly not with physically pursuing it. So far, petting had felt acceptable, but he hadn't been able to divest himself of the burdensome mindset that women having sex outside of marriage rendered them somewhat cheap.

Was all this mental agonising a valid way of coming to grips with complex issues, he wondered, or was it a way of drowning himself in complexities in order to avoid dealing with any of them thoroughly?

And what about his career, should he ever get out of this place? If he was to be capable of helping others, he would have to help himself deal with his anger and anxiety, his preoccupation with himself and the past. He had read that people could get so used to adversity that they then forgot how to live in its absence – that without realising it, they re-created or welcomed back conflict because that was the life they were used to.

The solution was obvious. He simply had to get away from all this turmoil by getting out of this hospital ward. He could not imagine staying for even a few weeks more, much less indefinitely. He was being knocked about by the medication they were giving him and struggled to behave well, wanting to give them no reason to restrain him or administer shock treatment.

It was scary; he could not stand the sound of shock treatment. Too much of his life had been spent fighting for survival, and he was tired of it. He knew that to be able to help others adequately, he had to firstly help himself.

One thing he was certain of: though non-observant as a Jew, when he got out, he had no intention of giving up the religion. This was what he'd been born into. It had not been removed by force during the Holocaust, and his religion would not be lost through indifference. He hoped one day to have a stable family life and to preserve the cultural aspects of being a Jew. He did not believe in God, but he did believe in treating other people well, in the way he wanted to be treated himself, and calling himself Jewish gave him a sense of belonging. He had also been told that he had what was referred to as a Jewish sense of humour. As far as he could ascertain, this was humour based on sending himself up, which, he thought, shouldn't be that difficult these days.

Thinking about being Jewish prompted Jerome to reflect on episodes of prejudice even in his own family. In Birmingham he had gone out a few times with a young woman named Tanya, a petite young woman with very blonde hair who was studying nursing. They had gone together to a wedding reception where his stepfather was also present. His stepfather had later phoned Jerome and abused him, accusing him of dating a non-Jewish girl, or a *shiksa* as he called her. Jerome was enraged at the prejudice, amazed that his stepfather, after suffering under the heel of anti-Semitism during the war years, could turn around and wield prejudice himself.

Jerome felt the old saying, *Sticks and stones can break your bones, but words can never hurt you*, was one of the most stupid expressions in common usage. He had no doubt that words could inflict a lot of hurt.

He did not let his stepfather off the hook by divulging that Tanya was in fact Jewish. Later, he would not let himself off the hook either – Tanya, although long departed from Jerome's life by that stage, would be one more person he felt he'd let down when he decided to break off with his previous life and go to America.

Episodes like this brought him back to the idea that everyone had the capacity to do evil, depending on the circumstances. The depth of anger and resentment that he harboured a lot of the time especially, troubled him. He reminded himself that there were people whose caring and kindness was exemplary, but was it possible even they could commit evil in certain circumstances? He and Tom had talked about how people who stood by when evil was being inflicted by others were just as evil themselves.

He had also read about psychopaths, people who were not motivated to alter their behaviour, no matter how cruel, and experienced no guilt over their actions. Psychiatrists felt these individuals couldn't be treated as there was no motivation for change.

He began to sense some of the limitations that could and did occur in psychiatric care. He recalled his initial reaction when he entered the psychiatric ward, of feeling that he was surrounded by aliens, beings he couldn't relate to. He realised that if he had not stepped back a bit and spent time trying to understand what everyone might be experiencing, then the barriers between himself and these aliens would have remained. It was only after he began seeing them as human that he began to commence the long process of understanding them as much as he could. He appeased his conscience by recalling scattered times when he tried to relate to some of the other patients, feeling them and himself, come alive.

Jerome recalled when he'd first heard of the catastrophic plane accident which caused the deaths of Klein and Anderson and his spouse, and how he'd reacted with overwhelming anxiety, his thoughts crashing in all directions. He had compared it at the time to a feeling he'd had when his mother died. But with his mother, there had been a strong sense of loss and regret over the pain she'd had to endure. Grieving over her loss was difficult, as he believed he had lost her years before, even prior to her personality being beaten out of her. Though consumed with anger, in the weeks that followed the loss of his mother, Jerome had battled his way through and had been quite proud of how he managed to contain his emotions to some degree.

His reaction to hearing about the deaths of the two doctors, he had to admit, was instead very much centred on the problems it created for himself, with no real empathy for the doctors' families.

Even now, he nurtured a faint hope that there might be someone who knew about the trial experiment. But deep down he remembered how the two doctors had stressed the secrecy of the set-up and their preference that no-one else have knowledge of it.

Now four weeks had passed and there had been no sign that anyone might rescue Jerome from his predicament. It continued to look as if the only person who knew he shouldn't be there was himself. He was starting to believe that evil could occur deliberately or by chance in equal measure.

Chapter 11

Days Unending

Early one morning, at breakfast, Jerome remained quiet, avoiding eye contact with anyone, but knowing his distress was evident to Tom, who sat beside him. Tom touched Jerome's hand and said in a gentle voice: 'There's something going on, isn't there? You want to tell me about it?'

'No, no, it will be okay,' began Jerome, before blurting out: 'You don't ever think about getting out of here Tom, do you?'

Tom put a finger to his mouth. 'Let's leave it for the moment.'

They ate in silence and afterwards slowly walked to the same wooden bench. It was in a pretty spot, but Jerome felt as if he was a weed amongst the bushes.

He turned and looked at Tom, who met his gaze. 'I've gotta get out of here. I feel myself going crazy. Then they'll have a right to keep me here.'

Jerome had become increasingly preoccupied with the thought that some of the hurdles he continually had to clear had been erected by himself, and he'd begun to wonder whether he had become addicted to living in that manner. Was it possible he needed to create such hurdles to feel alive? An answer was not forthcoming. His thoughts and emotions were racing in all directions, crisscrossing each other, and he felt totally washed out, with the day hardly begun.

As Jerome started explaining these feelings and concerns to Tom, his voice trailed off as he realised that once again, he was talking in a manner that only served to distance him from other people.

Tom, ever supportive, sensed this discomfort and gently put his hand over Jerome's clenched fist. 'It's okay, I understand.'

There was silence for a while, eventually broken by Jerome saying, 'I think you believe me, that I am not ill, but I'm never going to convince these jackasses.' Jerome fought back tears as he continued. 'You know Tom, if I escape from here, once again I will separate from a person I really care for. I've grown to feel really close to you and who knows when I might see you again.' There was another silence, then Jerome added firmly, 'I will see you, one way or another.'

Tom now spoke quietly, though not in an absolute whisper, not wanting to dramatise his words. 'Jerome, listen, I've got a small nest egg, a stash of money in here which I don't need because I'm certain that I don't want to be living out there. That money can keep you going for a while, even if for only a short while. The other thing I want to offer you is Ted.'

Tom grinned as he saw Jerome's reaction. 'You're wondering who the hell Ted is. Let's just say he is known to the police. He is tough and rough, but I have known him for years and I like and trust him. He's worked as a forger for most of his adult life, of which quite a few years were spent in jail. He can forge just about anything you might want.'

Jerome couldn't help wondering how Tom had developed such a close bond with an individual he was now essentially describing as a criminal. He decided he couldn't really pursue that query if he was to accept the offer of help from Tom.

Tom clearly felt he needed to provide further reassurance, because he added: 'I'm sure that if I refer you to Ted, he will be reasonable with what he charges you. Think about it, and after you and he talk, you may very well develop a new identity.'

Jerome felt a torrent of thoughts and emotions coursing through him, a significant part of it being excitement. But he tried to remain as calm as he could. A worrying thought that crept into Jerome's mind was that if Ted had carried out criminal activities such as forgery for a long time, what did that say about the money Tom was giving him now?

○

Jerome slept fitfully that night. Early the following day, Tom approached him and said in a quiet voice, 'I've thought about it further, about how you can best escape. You know the other wards in this hospital have far less security compared to us. If we can create some chaos in our ward, like triggering the fire alarms, there will be people running around in all directions, and firemen coming in and out, so that should give you a very reasonable chance of slipping out to one of the upper floors, given that none of the staff here apart from the matron are in uniform.'

The proposal made Jerome feel very anxious, but he made himself focus. The saying came to him, *Every saint has a past, and every sinner has a future.*

He looked at Tom and said, 'I can't begin to thank you. I'm already missing you.' After gazing for a while at the ceiling, he then said, 'I'm going to give you a poem I recently wrote.' He rummaged through his belongs until he found it.

What's in a label
we may well ask
Does it define the person
or rather the task?
Or does it generalise
to such a degree
that we're all labelled
and hung from the nearest tree?

Jerome then gathered himself and found a longer piece he called 'Opening and Closing the Gate.'.

Conceived in innocence
or conceived in rape,
both commence life
oblivious to their eventual fate,
yet commencing life with a clean slate,
in time becoming etched
with desire or even hate.
How do they learn the beauty of life,
avoiding the sewers of spite and hate,
continuing to live
with a clean slate?
Can they inhale
the scents that inspire,
and gently deal
with every urge and desire?
Is it a choice determined by them
regardless of things they hear and see
to keep their own slate clean,
potentially corrupted by images and words
from sources known and unknown
that can come to them unrequested or aware?
Is it predestined
without self-blame,

or do they alone determine
outcomes of fortune or feelings of shame,
possibly hoping their slate remains clean?
Yet if they sink
to the depths of despair,
was it their choice
to stumble and fall,
to learn to hate
without needing to think,
achieving a slate no longer clean?
So who took their innocence
and cast it aside?
They can no longer
hide nor blame
the people who preached,
telling them we were not all the same,
ready to accept that not all slates remain clean.
Yes, they heard preached a gospel of hate,
but it was they
who chose to open the gate.
They could have learnt
from others who cared,
and avoided dirtying
the slate that was theirs.
Instead of nurturing
the love and respect,
or retaining the capacity
to be kind and fair,
they somehow let the evil seep in,
creating the refuse
that was later recognised as sin,
and possessing a slate that would never be clean.
They could have learnt
from those who cared,
and nurtured love, respect and the capacity to be fair,

rather than seeking out differences that they could hate,
and standing idly by
whilst others suffered their very cruel fate,
ignoring how they had soiled the original blank slate.
And if they begin wondering
whether it's too late
to undo and repair the virulent hate,
beginning to wonder about blaming others
or whether to consider looking at self,
they come to the realisation that only this can allow
the cleansing of some of the slate,
letting them be free.
The awareness hits them
that it's gone too far,
as they look at the vision
of human remains with looks of despair,
eyes devoid of vision,
staring but unable to see.
People who have lost their identity to numbers engraved,
no longer surrounded by those they loved,
now just smoke in the air
They have little energy to love or hate,
their senses numbed, believing it's their fate.
Yet those in charge keep going ignoring these sights.
They avoid recognising remnants of those they'd been taught to
revile,
people who they were taught were evil, murdering our God, an
act of defiling.
They struggle to erase memories,
seeing them as subhuman, unfit to live.
So they are trapped with an image they can't bear to see,
leaving them without future and a hatred now of them and me.
They can't go forward, and they can't go back,
and there is no escape left for them or for me.
And when they are gone, what will be left to see?

Only wisps of smoke rising above nearby trees.
Too late they have realised they had a choice back then,
from the time they began walking
or the time they first held a pen.
They could have chosen to avoid this fate.
They could have avoided learning to hate,
and learnt instead when to open and when to close the gate.

Jerome smiled gently and said, 'Listening to a witness can make you a witness. I think Elie Wiesel said that.' He then explained to Tom how his poems related to what he and his family experienced during the Holocaust, and what he felt about the perpetrators of those horrors.

'I feel it occupies my mind too much of the time and I resent giving up that time,' he said.

Tom looked at him. 'I guess we've both discovered shit happens, often when you least expect it.'

Jerome felt lightheaded and confused, a headache attacking the back of his head. His clothes clung to his sweat.

Once again, he reassured himself that even though he did not believe in God as such, he would continue to feel Jewish and make it part of his cultural background. What they hadn't taken from him by force and fear he was not about to discard now.

Chapter 12

A few days later, Tom took Jerome aside when they encountered each other in a corridor. Tom opened his mouth to speak but suddenly closed it again as a staff member walked by. Jerome touched him on the shoulder reassuringly and said, 'Let's keep talking Tom. Like you told me once, they're not really interested in what we're saying, and it's probably as safe here as anywhere else to speak.'

Tom ran his tongue over his teeth and looked up and down the corridor, seemingly unconvinced that it was OK to talk.

Jerome filled the silence: 'I've been thinking about your idea, about creating a disturbance in our ward, and me going to one of the other levels to try and blend in with the staff. I think it'll work.'

Tom smiled before saying, 'I've already started setting it up Jerome. I've been collecting some paper from drawing supplies, gathering newspapers, and I've also put away a few boxes of matches. If we light the fire just before dinnertime, that should create quite a bit of confusion to mask what you're doing.'

Jerome felt uncomfortable about starting a fire, feeling the chaos could scare or even injure quite a few of the patients. He confided to Tom that he didn't feel good about that: 'I don't want anyone to get hurt. Their fear alone, thinking there's a fire, will be damaging.'

On the other hand, Jerome realised it was the only way he was getting out of there, and his own need to escape defeated the concerns he was expressing. He circled back to an earlier thought: everyone could do bad things depending on the circumstances, even he.

Some of the guilt at what the patients would be subjected to was partly diminished by learning the fire brigade had checked the fire alarm system recently and okayed it, as Tom told him. The fire was to be lit away from the sleeping area, and Tom said he would use slightly moist rags to create more smoke than fire, once they had been lit.

As the time approached for Jerome to make his move, the pressure showed, with rivulets of sweat running down his brow. He knew this move was not all gain. He was separating from someone who felt vital to him. He was flicking happiness out of his life, causing a wound that might be there forever. If he was honest with himself, he knew he and Tom were going in different directions. Tom would never want to live on the outside and Jerome would never want to live on the inside.

Jerome suddenly flung his right arm around the shoulders of Tom, drawing their bodies together, and he felt the moisture of his right eyelid brushing Tom's left cheek. As Tom moulded into the body and emotions of Jerome, he began to initiate the next phase of their movements.

His right arm firmly slid between their two bodies and with gentle but directional pressure got Jerome moving towards the exit. As they disengaged without a word or looking back, Jerome moved slowly and cautiously towards the still closed door and waited. It was close to 5:30 pm, when patients and staff gathered for dinner. This was the time Tom had chosen to spark chaos.

Tom now lit several matches and set fire to a pile of paper he had assembled near the entrance to the ward laundry, then threw some moist rags onto the burning pile. Soon enough, as the fire and smoke built up, a shrill siren sliced through the air, and patients began darting chaotically in all directions. Even the staff seemed disordered and fearful.

Jerome felt a twinge of guilt as he heard some of the patients screaming and saw several faces contorted with fear. He glanced at Tom, but his friend did not seem troubled, dispassionately watching what was happening.

As he watched the disorder build up, Jerome glanced one last time at Tom, then turned quickly and slipped into the bathroom, which was empty as he had hoped. He was grasping a laundry bag which held some street clothes belonging to Tom, from when his friend had first been admitted, and Jerome quickly changed into them.

At the bottom of the bag was a small bundle; the cash that Tom had stowed away. Jerome had left the door to the bathroom slightly ajar, and he watched the corridor keenly. He was waiting for the next large group of people to run past, whereupon he would join them. Within a few minutes, several individuals dashed past, and Jerome ran along behind them.

Firefighters moved about the hospital. They must have been in the vicinity of the hospital when the alarm sounded. The doors to Jerome and Tom's ward were normally secured, but as hoped, they had been flung open so that an emergency evacuation could take place. And it was a disorganised one at that. Fear had obviously replaced rational decision-making, with people running in all directions, seeking only to escape from the area. High-pitched screams pierced and were blood-curdling to Jerome's ears. He found it bizarre that there was no attempt at a cohesive, orderly evacuation supervised by staff.

However, he was amazed that the matron was nowhere to be seen. It could be she was positioned in some other area considered vital for the evacuation. The other strong emotion Jerome was experiencing was mixed with some degree of confusion that an apparently caring person like Tom appeared to have been comfortable subjecting so many ill and dysfunctional people to the fear this chaos was arousing.

Jerome himself initially felt guilty at subjecting vulnerable patients to so much chaos and fear but his own strong desire to escape allowed him to put those concerns aside. Once through the doors, Jerome considered sticking to the original plan, which was to go upstairs to the next ward, which served individuals who were less ill and where movement in and out was relatively unrestricted. But with adrenalin coursing through him, he made a snap decision feeling the sooner he had escaped the confines of the hospital the better were his chances of avoiding capture and being returned to his hospital ward.

He rapidly headed straight for the hospital entrance/exit, which sat wide open probably to allow free movement of the fire brigade.

Jerome had wanted to make for the boarding house on escaping, but Tom had talked him out of it. He'd argued that while Mrs Sykes appeared a kindly soul, there was a high chance that she would report Jerome's return to the police. This convinced Jerome to escape through the front entrance and go straight to Ted's home, the address of which was scrawled on a piece of paper in his pocket. He bolted out the front of the hospital building taking with him a flood of mixed and confused emotions.

As much as he could, he put them in an overflowing emotional bucket to deal with later. These intense feelings were a real mix of emotions and thoughts ranging from the guilt and discomfort of subjecting fragile human beings to intense fear, the impending loss of his strong friendship with Tom and realisation that what he was doing would be deemed a crime.

Jerome had not had time to give transport a lot of thought, and as he ran, he was thinking that he'd need to either catch a cab or hitch a ride.

Suddenly his right arm was seised in a firm grip, and an equally robust voice demanded to know what he was doing and where he was going. The voice identified itself as Bill Flint, a nurse from the third floor of the hospital. Jerome fought to control his fear and, locking eyes with his assailant, he introduced himself as Robyn Walter, a nurse from the second floor.

'Would you believe I started this job just under two weeks ago and this happens. Just got a call, my sister has been taken to Emergency at the general hospital. They don't know what's wrong with her at the moment but feel it's serious. Given the way I feel, I think it's better I catch a cab rather than drive.'

Bill Flint relinquished Jerome's arm, and with a sympathetic look on his face wished him and his sister the best. He encouraged Jerome to contact him when convenient and if he needed any support. They went in different directions, leaving Jerome to look up and down the main road, but unable to detect any cab. There did not appear to be a strong likelihood of catching a cab, so he chose the other option of hitchhiking. With thumbing a lift, he calculated that the odds of being identified as an escapee by the driver were minimal.

It was not the most logical decision, but Jerome believed that he had a reasonable feel for what people might be like, and so he began looking for a lone driver, with no other passengers.

After 15 or so minutes of walking, Jerome's thumb persuaded a car to pull over. It was an unremarkable-looking sedan, clean and without dents, and driven by a scholarly-looking man wearing glasses, aged about forty-five.

'Where are you headed?' the driver inquired.

Jerome snuck a look at Ted's address and repeated it aloud, explaining that he had been released early from a shift at the hospital because his son was ill with a bad stomach ache and needed him to come home. As he got into the passenger seat he noted the music playing on the car radio, which sounded like modern jazz, and he encouraged the driver to keep playing it at the current volume, desperate to avoid any awkward conversation.

The driver, Theo, turned out to be a pleasant man, not too inquisitive, and happy enough to listen to the music rather than probe into Jerome's history and personal particulars. And he was prepared to go a short distance out of his way to deposit Jerome at Ted's abode.

Jerome felt appreciative of the kindness of the man, firstly for picking him up and secondly for leaving him to his own thoughts without intruding. He started to feel he owed the driver the courtesy of talking to him. But just as he was opening his mouth, he recalled Tom's joking comment that people like he and Jerome had to live in a kind of hell when alive to compensate for missing out on it after they died. The thought of this made him feel that there was some benefit to the silence, as it diminished the risk of him saying more than he should Still, he was tempted to take the plunge, feeling that the driver had shown a generous spirit and he owed him the courtesy of conversation.

Jerome didn't feel he'd fully escaped yet. It had been well over a month since he'd been admitted to the ward, and so many things had gone wrong in that time. Now he'd lost Tom as well. And had he really gained his freedom? Apparently, he had, but he just couldn't feel any sense of relief.

The lyrics from Bob Dylan's *Neighbourhood Bully* came to mind, the lines about a man being outnumbered by a million to one, and how there was nowhere for him to escape to, nowhere to run. Although this rhyme obviously had not been written specifically for Jerome, there was a lot in its sentiments that he felt applied to him.

Jerome had written his own verses to capture the unfair, unequal battle he felt he'd had to fight by virtue of being different, by virtue of his religion, by virtue of the family he came from. The odds had always been stacked against him, or so he'd felt, reflexively shutting out any examination of his personal contribution to the situation. Those verses, to which he'd given the title **'Survival in spite of unequal odds'**, now came to mind as the car swept him towards Tom's friend.

I've spent my life running and hiding,
always pretending to be
someone different to the person they see.
My crime is not clear,
it never was.
They say guilty as hell
regardless of the cause.
I'm attacked from all angles
because they want me to live in fear.
My main crime appears to be that I exist,
and as long as that is, the hatred persists.
In turn I can pretend
that I'm not really there,
as if I've evaporated and fail to exist.
Yet they prime their weapons.
Is that really fair?
They never get to know me
nor do they bother to try,
to learn about the person I am,
not just a passerby.
They attack my religion
whilst pretending I'm not there,
telling me I fail to exist.
Yet to make me suffer
is something they continue with,
remaining highly motivated to persist.
They attack my religion,
yet pretend I'm not there.
I have spent my life hiding,
praying they won't dare.

They have never known me
for the person I truly am,
instead continuing to harshly judge me
as they run down my parents and religion, none of it fair.
I feel I am always on trial,
as if I shouldn't have been born.
I continue to be their daily target,
to be bashed and abused, leaving me smashed and forlorn.
There are few hiding places,
few means of defence,
nowhere to run or hide,
whether it be a hole or a fence.
What keeps me going is self-belief and drive,
determined to succeed and stay alive.
There is no way I'll let them crush me.
I owe it to myself and others as well
who may have fallen by the wayside,
forced to live in a version of Hell.

Jerome felt the odds had always been stacked against him, reflexively avoiding any examination of a possible personal contribution to these problems.

Jerome realised he was again locking himself into his own thoughts, communicating with himself alone, inundated by black images. It was a big step from knowing and controlling to changing that kind of thinking, but he believed that this might well be a crisis point in his life, and that it was vital he get on top of it.

Chapter 13

Theo took Jerome right to Ted's front door. Jerome thanked him for his kind support.

Ted lived in a modest cottage on the outskirts of Riverdale. The man who opened the front door appeared average, but the sparkling blue eyes hinted at a sharp mind at work. He was calm and hospitable, and Jerome was immediately fascinated as to why this man had been prepared to commit crime as a living in the past, and even now was using those skills on request.

Jerome had also begun to wonder further about Tom's background given his apparently close relationship with a man like Ted, who had what could only be called an active criminal background. Ted sat Jerome down and offered him a coffee. He gave the impression that Tom had fully briefed him, and that in anticipation of the work required, he had already set up photos and paperwork.

'So, Jerome,' said Ted, a grin flickering at the corners of his mouth. 'How would you like to be Lee Gold, eminent psychiatrist?'

He produced a short stack of documents, as if from thin air. 'Here's a passport, a graduation certificate from Toronto University, and a licence to practise psychiatry.'

Jerome was almost speechless as he looked at the immaculate forgeries, capable only of stuttering a thank-you. When he'd composed himself, he asked: 'Is there anything else I might need?'

'Well,' said Ted, 'I suggest you get yourself outfitted in a good suit, shirt, tie, shoes and so on, to look the way an aspiring psychiatrist would look.' He continued smiling as he informed Jerome that he had booked a flight for the following morning, which would take him to Melbourne, Australia. It was the first leg of a trip to the town of Katherine in the Northern Territory. He handed over the plane tickets and details of who to ring in Katherine – it seemed a job was available for a suitably qualified psychiatrist in the remote town.

Jerome asked how much he owed Ted for everything he'd done, to which his host responded with a modest figure of $340 which included the plane ticket cost, and a request for 'one hour of free analysis in the future'. Jerome thanked him and completed the financial part of the transaction.

He was ready to follow whatever Tom and Ted had organised for him, believing they had his interests at heart, but the question slipped out despite his trust. Why Australia?
Ted grinned. 'Well, probably several things make it a good choice. It's far away so less likely to be the place they'd expect you to run to. They speak ENGLISH. Symbolically it feels right as it used to be the place England deported their convicts to. And probably most important is that they are desperate for medical specialists in their smaller towns, so they don't look too closely at the paperwork you'll show them. The contacts I have there are dependable and will help you if need be. I had a network in Australia. They were well known to the police. I can't change that what we did was wrong in the eyes of most people. However, we didn't take from the poor and when we robbed the wealthy, we tried to focus on those who had accumulated

extreme wealth by exploiting others.' Ted gave a loud laugh. Even though the initial impression that Jerome had of Ted was relatively positive, he couldn't help but think that anything could be justified in this world.

Ted said he'd assumed Jerome wouldn't mind staying the night. He would then give Jerome a lift to the airport. Jerome felt embarrassed at the generosity being showered on him and realised Tom had played a part in it – a very significant part. There was no doubt in Jerome's mind about how close the bond was between Tom and Ted. In addition, Jerome wondered if there was also the appeal for Ted of the burst of excitement aroused by socking it to authority.

Jerome shared a light meal with Ted and his young Asian partner, Lina, and was about ready to fall asleep when, without warning, another young Asian woman appeared. She was very pretty and stood alongside Lina with her eyes downcast. Ted lifted her chin, revealing dilated pupils possibly connected with some degree of fear. Jerome felt aroused and at the same time guilty, anticipating where things were heading.

'This is Wu. She is yours for the night.' Ted smiled faintly as he made this announcement. 'I can see you are having a tug-of-war. I think you desire her, but you look shocked, too. Let me put it to you clearly. Wu comes from Asia and as a very young girl her family sold her into slavery. They were very poor and had gambling debts and could barely feed their four other children. From a very young age she worked as a domestic slave, was hungry most of the time, and as she got older, was repeatedly raped. When I bought her nine months ago, yes, she became a sex slave, but she is now well fed, no longer beaten, and is allowed money and clothing of her own. If she wasn't working as a sex slave for me, she'd be deported and would be treated far worse. You ask her if she prefers to return to Asia or stay with me.'

Ted locked eyes with Jerome and held a newspaper aloft as he said in a firm, calm voice, 'By the way, I just read that a nursing aid at your hospital, by name of Carlos, has been arrested on suspicion of doing away with you. Apparently a week ago, your landlady got anxious when you failed to return to the boarding house and didn't phone her. She couldn't reach you and checked with the hospital in case you'd been injured. They knew nothing about you – or at least, nothing about someone by the name of Brian. She feared something bad had happened to you, so she went to the police. This was about a week ago. The police became worried too, as doctors don't often disappear under the radar.

Ted grinned. 'You know, when Tom organised for me to help you out. I chuckled at the time, realising from the information he gave me that you'd had some past practice in changing identities.

'Now, there have been a number of violent crimes recently in the area around the boarding house, so a while back you as Brian and many others were hauled in and the police took swabs and documentation and filed it away.

Then recently another violent robbery occurred in the boarding house area and a black guy was reported running from the scene. So, the police dragged in a whole lot of black people, swabbed them and put it on file. There was a black guy Carlos who was a nursing aid at the psychiatric hospital who appeared to be carrying under his nails two lots of genetic data-one was his own and the second lot was someone else's genetic material. The police just filed it away and didn't attempt to investigate further.

'So when your landlady called the police expressing her concern about you, they finally checked their data and discovered in their files a description of a black nursing aide Carlos having two lots of genetic material under his nails. They discovered one lot matched that of Brian who was also on file.

As Brian had been reported missing, they hauled Carlos in and gaoled him on suspicion that he might be involved in your disappearance.

'I guess you know all this, well you certainly know now. You can see the confusion identity changes can bring about.

So I guess all you'd need to do if you wanted would be to go to the police and identify that you're the Brian they're looking for and Carlos hasn't done away with you. With a smile playing on his face Ted said 'I'd guess you'd rather not save Carlos that way, because they might drag you back to the hospital you've just escaped from.

Jerome didn't reply but knew Ted was right. He wasn't going to risk being forced back to the hospital he just escaped from.

He reflected to himself how he'd noticed Carlos being absent for a week or so but did not give it much thought at the time. He guessed Carlos acquired that extra genetic data when they wrestled or when he was asked to hold Jerome down for injection.

With a smile playing on his face Ted remarked 'I guess none of us are perfect. We all bend the law at times to suit our own needs.'

Jerome recalled a very short poem he'd written describing the colour related prejudice that black people were often exposed to, and how they risked being charged when a crime occurred.

They call me black as if it's a sin
They call me black –you can't come in
But it's a joke to look at them
They say they're white from head to hem
Hear what they say when sick with a cold
Or when they're close to 80 years old
Let them tell you their colour at birth
And if you saw them sunbaking, you'd be full of mirth
Colour shouldn't matter no matter the hue
But if it did, we remain black constantly, all of us, not a few
And Mr white man you change colour throughout your life
yet you pretend and accuse and cause the strife.

Jerome could not help but think about the query he had posed for himself a while back, as to whether all of humanity was capable of doing bad things or being evil at times. He'd collected and stored in his heart the identities of several people he felt he'd let down. Jill, Tom and Carlos were just the latest additions.

Brian recalled again that when he noticed Carlos was absent from work for a few days, he didn't feel it was of note. Holidays, a cold-who knows. He'll be back at work soon.

The saying entered his mind *we are all in the gutter, but some are looking at the stars*.

Ted, who'd stood back and watched as Jerome had interrogated his interior self, again spoke: 'So let me introduce Wu to you again. I hope you both have a pleasant night.' That night Jerome and Wu lay in the one bed Ted had provided. One part of Jerome desperately wanted to avoid what he knew would give him intense pleasure followed by the pain of guilt. Wu had been placed there to give him pleasure, but he was troubled by women that were forced into something they didn't want.

When he was in the hospital ward, Jerome relieved his sexual needs with masturbation and fantasy, and jokingly had the thought that the best way to stop that need was to visualise the matron lying alongside him. He saw the matron as an obnoxious creature who carried her job like a chronic disease never to be cured. At those times he visualised the fatty mass of a female, with glaring large red lips and blood shot eyes. Occasionally the image was the victor and sexuality lost out. This night, the quivering sensuality of Wu lying on her back and available for him readily won out as he rolled over, switched off the overhead light, briefly caressed the trembling flesh and gently entered her.

Chapter 14

Due to the skill of Ted, Jerome was now Lee Gold. He made a point of reminding himself that he would have to get used to responding to that name and offering it when required, as it was now his identity. But while he had escaped the psychiatric hospital and hopefully cleared yet another major hurdle in his life, deep down he knew he had not yet escaped from himself.

Yet again he was weighed down with a secret that he had to either keep hiding or lie about, and the knowledge that he had neglected and hurt people he cared about and had done so knowingly. There was no amnesia to hide behind. This could be added to things hidden in the past such as being Jewish or having alcoholic parents. Now having perfected the art of disguise he was about to hide that he escaped from a psychiatric ward and that he had no official training as a psychiatrist.

To some degree, Lee was now a stranger to himself – although truth be told, he had been for a long time. He longed for the day when his interactions with other people would not come with a built-in lie but with the truth flowing naturally. He recalled the old saying that one doesn't have to say everything, but what one does say should be the truth.

He let his body sink into his seat on the Qantas economy flight. The cabin of the plane was still dark, with the blinds down. It was close to 5 am – a red-eye flight. He had managed to sleep for a little, but having woken up, he now found his mind was too active to sleep anymore.

He was on the second leg of his flight from America, having had a stopover in Melbourne for several hours. Katherine had a population of just over 20,000, but this number swelled at various times because of an influx of grey nomads. Given that age group, the presence of adequate medical care had become even more important recently. Lee had rung Katherine Hospital as soon as he'd arrived in Melbourne and they had immediately given him an appointment, scheduled for an hour after his arrival.

When he landed in Melbourne, he had made good use of the money Tom had given him, heading straight for the shops in the centre of town, where he came upon what looked like an upmarket men's store. He had heard that Australian men liked to be casual in their attire, but from experience he believed that anyone in the position of hiring and firing tended to dress the part, like they did in England. So, in preparation for his interview, he dressed in a finely striped dark-blue suit, along with a white shirt and light-blue tie.

After touching down in Katherine, Lee checked into a motel as a temporary measure until he found an appropriate apartment, then he made straight for the hospital. The man who would be interviewing him was named Jeffrey Harris, and he was the clinical staff manager. As Lee entered the interview room, he had to contain a grin, noting that Harris was just as he had imagined him. The man was in his early fifties, neatly groomed in a suit to rival Lee's own. And he sounded more like an Englishman than an Australian.

Sitting there listening to Harris run through the duties associated with the position of psychiatrist at Katherine Hospital, Lee thought back to an old Jewish joke. According to Catholics, the foetus becomes a full human being at the moment of conception, but according to Jews, a foetus remains a foetus until it graduates from medical school. Lee decided it would be most unwise to bring this up. Harris didn't strike him as being into humour.

It was a Catholic hospital, but no questions were asked regarding his faith. In fact, few questions were asked about any aspect of his life, including his family or general background. Harris confined his queries to the year Lee graduated and where he had previously worked. In turn, Lee readily constructed the appropriate answers. It was apparent that the aim of the interview was not to seek obstacles to hiring Lee, but rather to minimise the risk of any obstacles arising that would get in the way of hiring him. After ten minutes, Harris stood up and announced to Lee – or Dr Gold – that he was hired, and the hospital was looking forward to having him work there. He said he would arrange an appointment for Lee to meet with the people responsible for paying his wages, probably the following day.

Lee would have liked to discuss what mental health facilities the hospital had - like the number of doctors practising as psychiatrists there and the number of beds available for patients -but he decided to leave all those queries for when he started. Like the staff manager, he didn't want to rock the boat.

And so there it was. Lee was now a practising consultant psychiatrist. He believed he could cope with the job and was determined to bolster his knowledge by asking for advice, going to lectures and seminars, and taking on any learning experience that he came across.

Dr. Lee Gold's caseload in the Katherine Psychiatric hospital appeared to consist of seeing, daily, the people who had been hospitalised in the psychiatric ward as inpatients. In addition to these ward consults, he was also scheduled to be available every day – or any time a further consult was indicated. An extra outpatient clinic was held twice a week which sounded somewhat sparse as described by Harris. And there was only one other psychiatrist at the present time. Roger had been employed in a similar capacity to Lee and would be working alongside him, or so Lee was told.

Though anxious about his lack of formal training in psychiatry, Lee knew he possessed some store of knowledge of the field. This had accumulated from extensive reading, and from giving a lot of thought to how one needed to relate to psychiatric patients. He had developed a strong belief in the importance of taking a comprehensive history, in not rushing the assessment and treating patients as human beings who had been injured in some manner. He also felt prepared to speak to psychiatrists with experience in the field and learn from their expertise.

Katherine felt more like a suburb than a town, and Lee wondered if everyone living there knew everyone else who also resided in the town. On the one hand that might feel cosy, but he imagined for some it could feel intrusive. He did enjoy the feeling of warmth on his skin, but anticipated that he might in time miss the variation of climate that many larger cities often had. That was his perception at least. Even the vegetation appeared somewhat uniform, cute at present, but could it become boring in time? Some degree of apprehension obviously remained in residence about the prospect of life in this small town, Lee felt.

Roger was quite elderly; indeed, he was due to retire in the next month or so as his health was rather poor. Lee had the impression that the hospital planned to replace the man with several fresh faces after he left. Within a short space of time, Lee also realised that Roger worked in a manner that would have suited Riverdale Psychiatric Hospital. Lee attempted to speak to Roger about a patient they were caring for, in the ward where they were both working. This was a middle-aged man called Pete who'd been in the ward for two years, without evidence of significant improvement.

Roger cut him off abruptly: 'Stop mollycoddling this guy. He's been here for ages without any improvement. You can't trust any history he gives you. It's not worth trying to take a history from him as it will be pure fiction. Or should I say *impure*.'

Lee stayed silent, tossing up whether it would be worthwhile trying to elicit more about the patient from Roger. Finally, he said: 'I think I know what you're saying Roger, but can you fill in a few gaps for me? Like, is he married, what work did he do before hospital, and what support people are in his life?'

Roger heaved an enormous sigh and replied, 'All you need to know is he's chronic. He's psychotic, and all we can do is give him medication to keep him calm and accept the fact that he's not going to change. Not for the better anyway.'

Lee vowed to himself he would find out more about this patient and spend some time establishing a rapport with him, having given up the notion he and Roger could work together. When he eventually attempted to talk to Pete on his own, he discovered it was heavy going. Pete was so deeply sedated with large doses of tranquilisers that he struggled to stay awake. However, Lee persevered and gradually began to reduce the man's medications. Then, lo and behold, Pete started grinning. He still had some screaming nightmares, but slowly an image of a human being, albeit a damaged one, began to emerge. Lee hoped that Roger would retire from the ward very soon, so he could then reduce Pete's medication even more.

In addition to the treatment of patients under his care, Lee had some teaching obligations concerning the medical students who rotated through the hospital. And he was further informed that in about a month, psychiatric lectures and seminars would be commencing that Lee could listen to, news he received with great relief.

Lee found that the knowledge he already had, supplemented by talking and listening to other doctors, plus reading up on psychiatric issues, allowed him to practise in a reasonable fashion. He concentrated on letting his patients speak, and taking their comprehensive histories. Lee was starting to find it hard to imagine what would cause the hospital administrators to fire him, as it was apparent that the last thing they would want to do was to terminate his employment.

And yet, thrilled as he still was at having escaped the closed psychiatric ward in Riverdale, he found himself unable to totally put aside his discomfort and occasional feelings of guilt at having left Tom behind. He missed having someone close by he felt secure with, someone he could confide in. Before his escape, he and Tom had decided that it would be unwise to try and communicate with each other in the first few months in case it led to Lee being traced, arrested, and brought back to Riverdale. But later, who knew what was possible?

To a lesser degree, Lee experienced some concern about a few of the other patients he had gotten close to in the Riverdale ward. He wondered how they felt about his getaway, and whether they deeply resented the panic he had created with the fire being lit. He was worried they thought badly of him for leaving so abruptly, not telling them what he planned, and judged him because he'd done it.

But Lee's greatest anguish was reserved for the predicament Carlos now found himself in. He tried to avoid thinking about it, though he could not always suppress the knowledge that he was betraying what was the ethical response. He had weighed up the implication of giving evidence to get Carlos out of jail, but knew it meant exposing himself; destroying any chance he had of pulling off the subterfuge of presenting as a fully trained psychiatrist.

Now that he had commenced working in the discipline of psychiatry– albeit he was proceeding cautiously – Lee found himself fascinated by the nature of his work. He felt that what he was doing was making a difference, a positive difference, in the lives of the people. He spent a lot of time listening to what the patients had to say, always keeping in mind he was dealing with damaged human beings who were suffering in their own way.

Gradually he got to know other medical staff too, both those who worked at the hospital and those who visited to consult. To the nursing staff working with and around him, Lee appeared to be gentle and kind, but this took a fierce struggle to achieve. The others had no idea about the waves of rage and turbulent fantasies that intruded on his everyday life, often at unpredictable times. These were feelings that he had to fight to control more often than he would like to admit, even to himself. These negative feelings weren't connected to the patients he was seeing but rather had to do with past traumas. He toyed with the idea of getting therapy himself, but he doubted it would be productive as there were essentials that he didn't feel he could reveal at this point.

How would he talk about the loss of family members during the Holocaust as a wave of barbarism swept over Europe, leaving him devoid of what he saw others enjoying? Family outings were not part of his existence. Not only were these people missing from his life, but he had no memory of them, had no photographs of them, nor even a grave that he could attend and pay his respects. It was as if they'd never existed.

He could probably talk about the experiences of bullying that he'd been subjected to. No youngster likes feeling different to their peer group, and he'd been very different, that he knew. He looked different, spoke differently, ate different foods, wore very different clothing, and his parents were unlike the parents of other students – he stood out like a neon sign. He'd asked himself what was wrong with being different, even as he knew the answer: that even though being different didn't necessarily equate with being inferior, that was how the other children judged it, making him the target of painful bullying.

The teachers saw him as being different as well, making no attempt to protect him, nor did they attempt to educate the other students to better understand and deal kindly with these differences. Once he got to high school, he was treated a lot better, and he felt he was more a part of the group around him. However, he was constantly aware that this acceptance was somewhat fragile and could always be shed.

It got him thinking about evil once again, and his belief that evil could occur anywhere, in anyone. He reflected on how Germany had had a high level of education at the time of the Holocaust. Thus, it seemed to him that education was not a guaranteed defence against savagery. So, what was a defence? He felt that role models and teaching in the family home were vital for generating caring attitudes towards other people, though there was no guarantee this would never break down.

Lee remembered reading and re-reading the parable of the Good Samaritan. He first came across this fable when reading Martin Luther King, who related how a severely injured man lay beside a road. Another man walked up to the wounded man and said to himself, 'If I stop and try to help this person, then what might happen to me?'

He decided to move on rather than risk being hurt. By contrast, when the Good Samaritan came upon the injured man, he said to himself, 'If I travel on and do nothing to assist this man, what will happen to him?' He decided to help the other man regardless of the risk.

Bitterly, Lee considered how he had not encountered any Good Samaritans amongst the people he'd dealt with after arriving in Birmingham.

It troubled Lee how frequently his thoughts and emotions were saturated by evil actions. He wished he could put some distance between himself and those notions and experiences before they overwhelmed him. However, most of the time, Lee was able to keep these negative contemplations under wraps, to bury them quickly whenever they erupted – still, once buried they could continue to fester away.

○

Lee was very excited when, a month into his tenure, a young anorexic woman called Felicity was admitted to the ward, though at the same time he was anxious as to whether he could treat her adequately. Ideally, he felt the ward could handle at the most eight inpatients with the current staffing arrangements, and he had been relieved to find there were only three inpatients when he commenced work. Regarding this new admission, he certainly felt that outside the hospital there was no way to help her control her anorexia, and that she would be highly exposed to the risk of becoming suicidal.

Felicity, aged 19, had a wispy figure and long light-brown hair, presenting a waif-like appearance that belied her age. She was like gossamer, Lee felt, and she made very little eye contact, avoiding it whenever she could. He gradually observed that she looked forward to conditions which allowed her to hide, whether it be the darkness of night or a severe storm where everyone hooded up. He learnt in time that her reluctance to look people in the eye was associated with her fear of seeing condemnation in their eyes. It was a feeling not unfamiliar to him.

Felicity had been seeing a psychiatrist for over a year on a weekly basis, all the time wondering why she persevered, as she felt she got nothing out of it. She answered her own query, believing that like everything else in her life, she did it because it was expected of her.

She had no friends, nor any significant acquaintances, and felt that wherever she ventured, she encountered groups who appeared to have a steely determination. By contrast, she felt she staggered from one day to the next.

According to the history she gave Lee, Felicity was an only child whose father had referred to her from a young age as a 'pretty thing'. Her mother was sullen and refused to dish out any compliments to her daughter, seemingly resentful of how Felicity received compliments from her father. The mother was clearly never a recipient of such praise herself. Felicity could recall her mother on multiple occasions telling her what a difficult pregnancy she had experienced, and how it made her decide to have no further children.

Her father would caress Felicity gently, and continued to do so even when her body was beginning to bloom. He would sit her on his knee and gently run his hands over the developing contours that she was now aware of. On occasion – in fact, on many occasions – he would laugh and give her a poke, telling her she was getting fat. A couple of times he remarked how large her breasts were becoming, and how people might think she was pregnant. He frequently told her that he didn't want her dating boys, as they were 'after only one thing'. But he also told her that when she got to sixteen, he would teach her how love should be done.

By the time she got to thirteen years of age, Felicity had started hating who she saw in her bedroom mirror. At first, she wondered if that particular mirror was the problem, but she soon discovered any other mirror she tried was the same. She did her best to suck in her breath, attempting to flatten out the contours of her body, but it made no difference. She started cutting back on what she ate and wearing tops she could hide in, but although she lost weight, it made no difference to how she felt about herself – she never seemed to lose enough. This pattern concerned many of the people who knew her, but not her. For the first time, she had power and people's attention, even though it was in the form of being overly concerned about her.

When her father died suddenly in a work accident on a building site when she was about 16 years of age, she felt as if she had lost the source of all possible joy. She was numb a lot of the time, to the point that even pain felt better.

Lee found himself putting a lot of time and effort into understanding and trying to help this young woman, while remaining aware that he had to be careful not to take on the special role that her father had adopted, to not be a rock for her to lean on excessively.

For Lee, treating this young woman was both confirmation that he could make a difference, and a lesson in the importance of striking a balance so that Felicity's illness did not become a source of satisfaction or pride in himself. Lee also got in touch with a leading authority in the field of anorexia nervosa and essentially had him monitor the therapy and approach Lee was adopting in treating this young woman. He did have to contend with some of the staff feeling that he was indulging her, that all she had to do was pull herself together and be discharged, but he gradually began believing in himself, feeling that he was slowly learning how to be an effective and good therapist.

Even though Lee was aware that Felicity would require a prolonged period of hospitalisation, it did not feel as if she was vegetating. There were signs of gradual progress, though the risk of her giving up still blotted the overall picture. What particularly impressed Lee was that Felicity was becoming positive about her progress. Also, some of the clinical staff began to feel her treatment was proving worthwhile and became more positive and supportive about the approach being used to treat her.

When Lee compared all of this to what he had noted in the ward at Riverdale, he began to feel that the ward at Katherine Hospital had a sense of life about it, that hope coursed through its veins. He could see this in the way the patients interacted with each other, rather than being locked within themselves, oblivious to the outside world.

Lee had to battle some of the hospital's bureaucracy, who tended to be guided by mathematical formulae when it came to deciding how long a patient admission should last.

Gradually Lee felt increasingly positive about what he was learning in treating patients, even though the approach was not as structured as he might have hoped and was something he was creating from many sources. He felt determined to persevere and to continue developing his career to the point where he felt that he was shaping events in an organised way, rather than passively waiting for life challenges to occur and hoping he could deal with them.

Lee pondered the irony of how he had recently been a patient when there was nothing seriously wrong with him, and now he was acting as a psychiatrist without having earned that qualification. Here he was attempting to help patients deal with reality, when so much of his own life had been devoid of it, and required the use of secrets and lies.

Underlying this approach was a current of fear, stemming from the knowledge that in treating patients in the role of a qualified psychiatrist, he was performing an illegal act in the eyes of the law. If something went wrong and a patient got sicker or, Heaven forbid, they died, then whether it was due to negligence on his part or not, he would be charged. What he was doing was a crime – there was simply no denying that.

That thought ate away at him – one night he dreamt about himself standing in court, handcuffed, being cross-examined by an aggressive lawyer – but he was determined to continue treating patients as if he was a trained professional psychiatrist. He made sure that whatever treatment was required according to his assessment, he would check and double-check it, including speaking to specialists.

Helping his general disposition, Lee found himself enjoying spending time in the first-floor psychiatric ward, where a nurse by the name of Penny worked. It had been a long time since he had last experienced such strong positive feelings towards a woman. When it came to other people he'd met, in the recent past, he'd tended to be more aware of a rumbling of irritation and anger inside him, fearful of eventual rejection by them.

In his calmer moments, Lee craved the opportunity to develop a long-term relationship, and perhaps one day to share children and his entire life with a partner whom he deeply cared for. But he also wondered if this was just a fantasy, and whether he was deluding himself. He knew that if a relationship was to develop with Penny, then no matter how close they became, there would still be the barrier of an underlying element of deceit or lie, as he could never fully share all his life with her.

He tried to stand back and assess what drew him to Penny. There was no doubt her interest in him and the small indications she gave of liking him helped. Whilst these reactions might have helped him feel safer, it was her eyes and sense of humour, her vitality and warmth and an element of insecurity in her makeup, that really appealed to Lee. It took him some time to realise how attractive her eyes looked when she was relaxed.

With partners he had cared for in the past, there had been performance anxiety at times. What if he didn't get an erection? What if she didn't enjoy the things he was doing? To him, it all seemed much easier for women, who could always just pretend they were turned on. Sure, there were signs like moisture, nipples becoming erect, skin flushing. But that was nothing like the neon light of men's arousal. Perhaps this was why, one night, he actively fantasised making love to Penny, to explore his readiness.

Lee had finished work for the day and returned to the apartment he'd recently begun renting, where he sat in a recliner. With closed eyes, he imagined caressing Penny's face as he guided her hand to assist him. His desire was great. And yet he was very aware that dreams could become the stuff of nightmares.

Lee believed that to many, Penny was an average person – average appearance, average height, average looks. She was a person whom many could pass on the street and not even notice, not until they'd gotten to know her better. But he'd seen many subtle, appealing qualities. She wasn't cruel. Was that the same as being kind? And had a quirky sense of humour that was easily encouraged. On one occasion, as they sat comfortably together on some grass near an oak tree, out of nowhere she said that it reminded her of something Spike Milligan had said, that the best cure for seasickness was to sit under a tree.

Penny had been married once, but the relationship had ended years ago, and it was not something she was keen to talk about. There had been no children, and that whole period of her life seemed to belong in a land of vagueness. Penny's body and voice were flat, very much as the curves of her life had been flattened out. She tended to keep her feelings to herself, as Lee's own mother had. Also like his mother, Penny appeared to be a recluse, a somewhat withdrawn person who avoided eye contact. She had a range of phobias and performed rituals that made her feel safer.

When he thought about it, Lee couldn't really explain what he liked about her, but it certainly went a lot further than merely feeling pity for what she was going through. He believed that deep down she would not hurt people deliberately, although most of her kindness seemed to be delivered to cats and dogs, a few of which she owned. Lee preferred being with her when no-one else was around, and he was tickled when he could get her to smile or to occasionally giggle. There was no doubt he felt safe with her, and he didn't feel as if he was competing with a multitude of men for her affections. He wondered – was it love or safety that drew him to her?

She was almost guaranteed to smile when he described incidents in which he showed himself to be a klutz. He had to translate the Yiddish word for her, which meant a clumsy oaf, and waited for her to reassure him that he wasn't like that. He explained that he saw her being like himself at times, which might be labelled as 'different'. He said that he believed many people had little tolerance for those who were 'different'.

Lee also shared how strongly he felt that one should have the right to be different if that difference did not hurt other people. It moved him to reflect on how unfair the labelling of people was. If one was wealthy and different, then the label might be *eccentric*, but if one was poor and different, they were more likely to be labelled *crazy*. He secretly wondered if part of Penny's appeal was that her eccentricity might cause other prospective partners to be very cautious in approaching her.

While Lee's confidence was still fragile, he found that it was building up through his experiences with Penny. He began feeling less awkward relating to people at work and started developing several superficial friendships. He had long believed that misery loves company, but now he was discovering that happiness does too.

Chapter 15

Just when things appeared to be on the rise for Lee, changes were pending that he was unaware of - changes that threatened to undermine the sense of wellbeing that had developed around him.

Back in Riverdale, Ralph Klein, son of the deceased Dr. Ludwick Klein, had decided that it was time to sort out his father's final will and testament. Lying in his bed alongside his sleeping partner, Ralph tried to rub his face into wakefulness, at the same time pondering the situation that now confronted him.

Ralph had not been to the family home for over seven years, having had a falling out with his parents many years back. The trouble in his relationship with his parents, especially his father, was long standing.

Ralph was the older of two boys and was now aged 31, whilst his younger brother Lesley if alive, would be 29. Their parents had a poor and unhealthy marriage, separating eight years before. Even when they were living under the one roof, they were separated emotionally.

In the years that followed the separation, a number of relatively young women came individually and shared the father's bed for varying periods of time. There was no sense of permanency, nor any interest in taking on the role of stepmother to the boys.

The father's disapproval of Ralph had begun earlier in his life, however. There was nothing that Dr. Klein could find to praise about Ralph, either academically or physically. Rather, he'd made it clear that he could not bear looking at his lump of a son, and that he expected less than nothing from him.

Finding Ralph so unappealing probably contributed to his father beginning to have doubts, where he increasingly wondered if Ralph was a product of an extramarital affair his wife had.

It said something for his attitude and the person he was that Dr. Klein decided not to do genetic studies, choosing to have the suspicion linger rather than risk finding out that biologically he and Ralph were related.

This way it left the possibility that Ralph was conceived outside of the marital relationship, and his father didn't have to face that his genes contributed to the lump he disowned.

So, Ralph had felt unloved by his parents for a long time – his mother Sylvi, had never really approved of him either – and truth be told, he did not particularly like himself. Biologically, he was not blessed. His eating patterns were guided not by quality or taste but by quantity alone. His body shape was testimony to this, his ever-swelling features failing to meet the criteria for the term *good-looking*. Obesity enveloped him in cascading rolls of fat, removing the demarcations normally evident in the human body.

He also had a face that only a mother could love, not that his had. He started avoiding mirrors, except when shaving necessitated using one. He tried not to look at other people's faces, so that he did not have to see their disapproval. Daily he swam in a sea of anxiety, trying to avoid drowning in it. But it was a face he was stuck with, much as a Bull Terrier is a slave to its own features and personality.

He would remark bitterly at times that his face scared the shit out of people, mainly because of the bulbous mass of a nose that dominated it. Ralph attributed his appearance to genetics, refusing to admit that he'd ravaged his own body with chain smoking, alcohol abuse, a diet of excess and little sleep.

He developed the habit of frequently elevating one arm, so it partially hid some of his facial features.

Ralph's brother Lesley was a year and a half younger than Ralph, and though he possessed many of the features that Ralph lacked, he also ran into multiple problems. He was good looking and athletic but went downhill like Ralph. Though the boys deteriorated in a similar fashion, they largely lived quite independently of each other.

What their father refused to face was that a major part of the boys' problems arose from the atmosphere at home and the destructive relationship their parents had.

In brief moments of honest reflexion, Dr. Klein admitted to himself that the home environment was toxic. Also, in even briefer moments, Dr. Klein asked himself how it was that he could help patients see the problems in their relationships, very often able to assist them in finding ways to improve, yet could not do that for himself.

In an atmosphere lacking in affection and support, both boys ran into problems with the police.. They both separately joined street gangs, had a range of charges and convictions connected with brawls and theft. Because of their father's influence in the community, both boys continued to avoid gaol.

They each had numerous car accidents, and one led to Lesley losing the use of his non-dominant arm.

Though he had lost contact with Lesley many years back, Ralph heard that Lesley was deceased and had died about six years ago from stab wounds in a street brawl involving rival gangs. He made no attempt to locate where Leslie was buried.

Sylvi broke away from the nightmare of her home and about eight years ago fled to her country-of-origin, Turkey. She had a period of psychiatric care based in a town where she was unknown. In her mind, as a desperate measure to survive, she made the decision to totally divorce herself from her two sons and her husband. By then, being in the vicinity of her husband aroused only fear, bitterness and anger. The mutual affection from the early days of their relationship was long gone. Any positive feelings about her two sons had been sucked away in a family where the pathology of the interactions left no room for caring about each other. It had been a marriage that became devoid of affection and at times deteriorated further into violence. Sylvi no longer felt like a wife or mother, believing the only way she could exist was by casting adrift marriage and motherhood. Not that her husband saw this as a loss. The children had difficulty remembering the mother they had.

The discrepancy between what patients of Dr. Klein were assisted in seeing as ideal in family life and what had occurred in his own family, defied belief.

The society that Sylvi fled to was less than supportive, but fortunately there she had a paternal aunt who took responsibility for caring for her. She now lived in an area where no one aside from the aunt knew her predicament, and this diminished the pressure for the time being.

At the time her ex-husband Klein died, she had already lost her marriage, lost her role as wife and mother, but avoided losing her life in a plane accident.

Ralph pushed himself out of bed so he could freshen up following a night of heavy drinking, in which he'd been joined by his partner. His plan was to go to his late parents' home first, and then to the office of his father's solicitor. He began priming himself to convincingly pretend that he missed his parents and was devastated by his father's death.

An hour later, he arrived at his parents' home, which was in a much better part of town, quite a distance from his apartment. He entered the sprawling house with a spare key his parents hadn't known he'd kept, then took a little while to orient himself before locating his late father's study, where he began leafing half-heartedly through piles of paper stacked on a leather-topped desk. As he read, he scowled, responding to a range of less than happy memories about growing up in this house. He recalled the saying that psychiatrists brought up their children by the book. *Some book,* was his silent retort.

He was in the middle of a yawn when he spotted it, and his head suddenly shot upward, a broad smile entering territory that was foreign to that type of expression. He rubbed his eyes to clear them and gave a low whistle. He had just read his father's description of the trial that Ludwick Klein and Stephen Anderson had set up in Riverdale's psychiatric ward. Ralph had not heard any mention of it in the media, which was good. The fewer people who knew about it, the greater the chance that he could leverage it for his own purposes.

By lunchtime he was sitting in the rather plush offices of his family's long-time solicitor, with its heavy antique furniture, impressive shelves of books, and a nice view over the town centre. The solicitor handed Ralph some paperwork to read. As far as he could tell, it appeared his parents, or rather his father, had left a considerable amount of money to charity and only a small amount to Ralph. There was no mention of the mother in the will. He couldn't help but notice that even the paltry sum left to him was subject to conditions, enforceable by the solicitor, that were aimed at preventing Ralph from dissipating the money through gambling or excessive drinking.

Ralph was very irritated – even in his afterlife, his father was treating him with scant respect. However, he had no choice but to go along with it for the time being and allow himself some space to think about other options.

While reading the paperwork, Ralph had noted there was no mention of the experimental trial his father had set up, except for a vague reference to using a young, recently graduated doctor from overseas, who wanted to study to become a psychiatrist and who would not be well known locally. He inquired of the lawyer whether the trial was continuing, and if so, who was now supervising it. The solicitor, who knew nothing of the arrangement, said they would check it out.

Over the years, Ralph had often been relying on welfare payments and had only found occasional work as an unskilled labourer. He had thought about becoming a trained nurse, like his partner, but had only done the odd shift in hospitals, infrequently playing the role of a nursing aide when they were short-staffed. What with the ongoing conflicts between himself and his parents, and his growing resentment and anger, he tended to look for activities that he knew they would disapprove of. So, a few years ago he'd joined what he termed the 'other side', an organisation – more like a sect, actually – that was virulently opposed to the career his father followed. In other words, they were vehemently anti-psychiatry. Ralph had become involved with Syntology to flag his defiance of his parents.

As the meeting with the lawyer wound up, with Ralph receiving a paper copy of the agreement, he wondered what his buddies at the head office of Syntology could do with this information about a secret trial. He was keenly aware that the thrust of a lot of their material was the inadequacy of psychiatry, and how many people in psychiatric hospitals in actual fact had very little wrong with them. As his father's experiment had been focused to some degree on highlighting the possibility of inadequate functioning of psychiatrists in hospital settings, and the inept way they might assess new patients, he believed his contacts at Syntology's head office would welcome receiving ammunition like this.

○

Later that afternoon, as Ralph sat in his car in the street outside his apartment, he rang the Riverdale Psychiatric Hospital, introduced himself to a member of the institution's administration, and inquired how his father's experiment was going.

'What experiment?' was the woman's puzzled response.

Hanging up, he again read through the paperwork he'd retrieved from his father's house, this time more carefully, and realised that only three people had been aware of the trial. These were the two head psychiatrists, and the young doctor about to commence psychiatric training. Now only one was still alive.

'With no one to back up his story,' Ralph said to himself smilingly, which presented as a sneer.

What caught his attention especially, was the fact that this patient Jerome Silver was a fictitious character with a made-up history. His real name was Brian Wright, as documented in his late father's paperwork at home.

He called back the hospital administrator and apologised for his earlier confusion, explaining that it was difficult to think clearly following the death of his parents. She expressed her condolences and said the plane crash had been a tragedy. Ralph chuckled inwardly when she spoke of his father being a wonderful man, adding, 'I guess you already know that.'

Ralph then told the woman that his father's notes seemed to indicate that he was particularly concerned about the psychiatric state of a patient called Jerome, and he said that he too was wondering how Jerome had dealt with Dr. Klein's death.

There was silence from the other end of the line, and then the woman explained to Ralph in a hesitant voice that Jerome in fact had absconded from the hospital sometime after hearing that Dr. Klein had died. She said that staff were very concerned about him and had informed the police, who had been searching for the man but without success. As he had initially come from overseas, the police suspected that he may have left the country, but his name had not shown up in the records of outbound flights or sailings.

It was now apparent to Ralph that the hospital had no inkling that the whole situation to do with Jerome had been contrived. He thanked the administrator for assisting him and terminated the call.

As he looked up and down the street, Ralph chortled to himself as he realised that the staff had no awareness of Jerome not really needing psychiatric care. He smiled to himself in anticipation of the thanks he would get from the senior people at Syntology, and how they would handle the information. He could imagine them running material through the media in a variety of ways. The headlines would emphasise how medically trained psychiatrists had admitted someone to their ward who had a false name and a made-up history, and psychiatric staff had failed to realise there was nothing wrong with that patient. The media would go to town on this, disclosing the inadequacies of the profession.

Ralph began mentally writing some headlines, settling on *"One man's normality is a psychiatrist's insanity: How psychiatry never runs out of patients."*

'Maybe,' he thought, 'the big boys in the head office would treat me with some respect now.'

He now set himself two goals. One was to work out how to access more of his parents' money for his own use, and the other was assisting the people at Syntology to construct the bullets they would soon fire repeatedly at the body of psychiatry.

If he couldn't get his father feeling under attack, then at least he could shred his reputation. He made room for this thought to sit in his mind.

Chapter 16

Lee had now been working as a consultant psychiatrist in the Katherine Hospital for close to a month, and he was gradually getting the feel of what he needed to do. As much as possible, he made sure that he did not go beyond his capabilities, and he consulted freely with more experienced psychiatrists and attended whatever lectures and seminars he could. He felt he was able to perform adequately and safely – even if the fear of being discovered and subsequently deregistered or otherwise punished was ever-present. And he found that most of the patients were appreciative of the time and effort they felt he was committing to his work.

The variety of problems in his patients fascinated Lee. He had begun treating a 40-year-old lady called Alice who had a marked phobia centred on birds, especially the fluttering of their wings. The condition was severely incapacitating, and initially he couldn't imagine what had brought this on. Once, as Alice walked along a garden path in the grounds of the hospital where Lee was working, headed for Lee's office, several birds suddenly took off from a nearby lawn. This was sufficient to cause her to run screaming into the medical building, in turn frightening many other patients in the waiting room. Fortunately, Lee had committed himself to taking a comprehensive history of every patient, and in Alice's case, it did not let him down.

The history he obtained, revealed that in Alice's adolescent years she had lived with her parents and younger sister in a home that was very basic, the wooden frame rotting in places. The only toilet facilities were outside, close to an extensive aviary which was her father's passion. He was in there most of his waking hours, avoiding his wife and the need to assist the struggling family. He had been out of work for many years.

Thus, when Alice went to the toilet, her father was nearby, and he progressively came closer and closer, until all privacy was lost. Alice's father went from inappropriately caressing her, to sexually molesting her. Alice didn't feel she could tell her mother, who could barely cope with day-to-day life as it was, and she was fearful of telling anyone outside the family. She attempted to use toilet facilities outside of home but could not always manage to do this.

Once Lee understood what had happened, it became a complex matter of approaching therapy with a family orientation and looking at legal avenues that could be used to assist the unfortunate Alice.

The need for flexibility and willingness to devote time to the needs of a patient at a particular point in time was highlighted with an incident involving Alice.

Lee had investigated the possibility of a desensitising procedure with Alice in his rooms. He put to her the following to think about as a possibility. He explained to Alice that if she was able to bring one of her father's birds caged into therapy, they could use it to slowly enable her to be around birds with much less anxiety. The following sessions of therapy that Alice had with Dr. Lee Gold, she came carrying a bird in a cage.

Over the initial sessions the bird remained in the cage, at times squawking and Alice seemed to handle it reasonably well. There was still some anxiety but not overwhelming.

Finally, they reached a point after several sessions where Dr. Gold encouraged Alice to open the door of the bird cage a crack so she could insert her hand and stroke the bird.

In theory this was the correct approach for desensitisation, to develop gradually and allow her to be around birds without the overwhelming fear of the past. Unfortunately, Alice accidentally opened the bird cage door too far and the bird escaped, squawking. Loudly. It felt to Alice like things were out of control again. She panicked and ran screaming out of the room, emptying the waiting room of patients waiting for their appointments,

Lee believed that it was important to secure the bird. For the next hour and a half, he and a nursing aide scattered bird seed around the consulting room and finally were able to capture the bird and cage it once more. It caused some degree of chaos with his appointment schedule that day.

Alice had been encouraged to stay in the building and was given medication to help calm her panic attack. Dr. Gold explained to her that their goal of desensitising her was still feasible and they would help her find a birdcage more suitable in the future and proceed slowly.

The staff were very impressed at Dr. Lee Gold's patience and willingness to give the patient so much extra time.

On another occasion, staff at the hospital were particularly impressed by what occurred with a 28-year-old man called Rick, whom Lee had begun seeing as an outpatient.

Rick, who came in on a weekly basis, had already been diagnosed with chronic schizophrenia. One morning, as Lee was about to usher Rick into his consulting rooms for an appointment, Lee suddenly felt extremely uncomfortable. On the spur of the moment, he persuaded Rick to go to the admissions section of the hospital and told him that once he was admitted, Lee would come and talk to him in the ward.. Rick followed those directions, and when Lee came to the ward to speak with him, the staff on duty said Rick had been carrying a butcher's knife which he had voluntarily handed over. He'd told the nursing staff a voice had been telling him to kill Lee, while another voice told him not to.

Though shaken by this incident, Lee was impressed by his own ability to sense how disturbed and potentially threatening this patient had been. Luckily, it appeared that the urge to harm Lee had been pretty much balanced by the urge not to.

Just as Lee was beginning to feel that his life was settling and some permanency was developing, with work going well and his social life becoming more stable, he received a letter from Penny explaining that she had departed from the ward and would now be absent from his life as well. She apologised for any hurt her decision caused Lee, but emphasised that it was a permanent decision, and she did not want to negotiate or discuss it any further.

In her letter, she said she liked Lee a lot but could not cope either now or in the future with the lifestyle that he was seeking, of having a family structure and children. She said that if he cared about her, he would respect her wishes and not pursue it further. She begged him to read what she had written and not attempt to find her, write to her, nor try to speak to her any further.

He eventually heard from a nursing friend of Penny, Odette. A week earlier, Odette had come across Penny in a flood of tears. This occurred in the staff coffee lounge, where Odette had heard her friend's agonising cries of distress. She held Penny for a short period until Penny broke loose and ran to the toilet. Behind the slammed door she heard fragments of Penny's voice.

'I like you Odette but I'm ashamed about what I'm feeling. Things have happened over the years that stop me, always will stop me, from living a normal family life. I can't be the person Lee is looking for. I need to leave this job and town and find a life I can handle. Please help me by trying to understand. When I settle down in a new place I might try and get some help. If you care about me you won't try to stop me. When things are calmer, I'll write you.'

In the past, Lee would have taken total blame for the break-up of the relationship, but now he was able to realise that Penny, like himself, had suffered considerable trauma over the years, and this had left her unable and unwilling to do some of the things that were necessary to build the lifestyle that he wanted for them both. Penny was heard saying that she wished they could go back to the beginning of their lives and start afresh, but obviously that was not possible.

They shed tears miles apart.

O

Though Lee felt shattered by the loss of his relationship with Penny, at some level he had always expected to lose the things he really wanted. He pushed himself through gritted teeth and began allowing himself opportunities to socialise. Bit by bit he felt himself becoming calmer, though he remained cautious in how he mixed with others.

He'd been traumatised by the break-up with Penny and felt sad for both of them, although he understood that Penny had not backed away from him but rather removed herself from a lifestyle she felt she couldn't sustain.

And so, despite this loss, or possibly because of it, a month later he found himself becoming increasingly attracted to a nurse called Gillian, who worked in one of the wards occupied by some of his patients. Her blonde curly hair and vibrant blue eyes caught his attention. The warmth of her smile and her easy-going nature soon prompted his body and mind to relax to some degree, not that his body and mind remained obedient at all times. However, he was willing to take some degree of risk as he knew from the past that to avoid risk could only lead to stagnation in a puddle of misery.

After a month of regular contact, Lee believed his feelings towards Gillian were genuine and valid, and mutual. Unfortunately, an age-old feeling returned. He found that the more he desired Gillian, the greater became his fear of losing her. It had happened too often in the past. He would smile and nod as Gillian spoke, while under his clothes, sweat accumulated in great quantities. A wave of sadness rolled over him as he couldn't avoid being aware that once again, he was hiding part of himself. He recalled with discomfort reading somewhere a saying: *The truth has no defence against a fool determined to believe a lie.*

He didn't believe the statement to be accurate in all situations. Gillian was no fool nor was he, but when a person cares about someone they tend to assume that person is being straight and honest and it comes as a shock if they ever discover that is not so.

'Maybe, just maybe, we can get so close that I can take the risk of opening up to her,' his mind said to himself yet again. Then the other part of his mind reminded him how his style was that the closer he got to someone, the more threatened he felt about the risk of rejection and losing that relationship.

One day they both finished work and, as the sun was still out, they strolled around the arid but lovely grounds of the hospital. Gillian led him to a pile of flat rocks, a secluded area that few people came to, and together they gazed out on a rapidly flowing watercourse. Lee was keen to learn more about Gillian and her family. The things she began to tell him appeared straightforward, but he knew that no family history is uncomplicated.

She described how her origins were a mix of American and Scandinavian ancestors, and though she had a Christian background, religion did not appear to have had a significant role in her life or that of her parents. She comfortably described how her father had been a labourer on the railways whilst her mother performed home duties, which were considerable as she had five children close together in age. Although in financial terms the family was poor, they had created for themselves a warm and supportive environment.

Lee felt an envy that he kept under wraps at first, as Gillian described a family situation which he had lacked in his own early life. It even gave him some confidence that she was less likely to bolt at the suggestion of one day building a family life together along similar lines. But eventually he felt he had to try and explain that, in comparison to the family tribe that had gathered on weekends and smothered Gillian with comfort, Lee had lost his grandparents to murderers during the Holocaust, and his youngest years were orchestrated by his parents with the sole aim of survival.

Again, he relived some of the trauma of the years during the Holocaust. Whilst he did not want to dwell on that, he believed she needed to know where he was emerging from if she was to have a chance of understanding where he was at now.

He showed her a photo taken after they escaped the labour camp and were living in Warsaw.

As they gazed at him sitting with a group of children from the kindergarten, he pointed out this happy, chubby child dressed as a mushroom. Neither of them spoke for a short while until his sadness and anger seeped through.

'There I am looking happy and the same as the other kids. What gives anyone the right to pinpoint me as the one to be eliminated. I'm not vermin, but all they need to know to get a green light to get rid of me is that I'm Jewish.'

He had reassured Gillian early on, rather cryptically, that he did not want her to feel uncomfortable about having had something that he desired but had missed out on. He just wanted her to understand a bit more about his background. As he was saying this, Lee felt amazed that he was letting so much pour out at such an early stage of the friendship. He had realised it was time to let himself share much more.

As he held her close to him, their cheeks brushing, he said in a soft voice, 'I don't want you to feel sorry for me or uncomfortable about the things that I'm going to tell you.' As he hesitated, Gillian gently put her hand on the back of his own, as if to say: *I understand, and you can trust me.*

His eyes downcast, Lee confessed that his real name was Brian, and then told Gillian that nearly his entire extended family had perished in the Holocaust. He personally felt it did not warrant having the dignity of a name applied to it.

He said that his parents had told him very little about those times, that most of what he knew had come from records in places such as Holocaust centres, like the one in Washington, and in dribs and drabs from various sources which he had carefully verified.

Brian said it was an ongoing dilemma for him; whether he had the right to be angry at the behaviour of his parents, or if he should make allowances because of the trauma they went through during the war years. Was it their Holocaust experiences that created the way they were and the things that pissed him off at times? One thing that annoyed him with his parents was their refusal to tell him the whole story, adding to the difficulty he experienced in knowing where to put the blame.

In the days that followed, Brian and Gillian shared a multitude of words and emotions.

One day as they lay together on a bench in the garden, they were stretched side by side and Brian could feel Gillian's warmth flowing, enveloping them both.

He felt she didn't need to say much as her body spoke for her, especially her eyes. They would light up accompanying her smiling lips.

As they lay close physically and emotionally, he detected the fragrance of cinnamon, but chose to not mention it yet.

Brian's soft voice told her she did not need his permission for anything she did.

She grinned. 'You're sure about that? I could put that to the test.'

Brian in a soft voice began to describe losing his father at a young age and the progressive damage inflicted on his mother by alcohol and a violent subsequent partner. He admitted in a choked voice that he had lost her long before she died.

He told Gillian about being born in Warsaw, which he figured was about the worst possible place to be born in at that time, and about the labour camp he'd been sent to. He said he couldn't understand why such a young child had been allowed to live in a place where it couldn't be productive, adding there were many things he couldn't understand and probably never would.

Brian knew Gillian to be gentle and kind and interested in people, even now, even as he was describing an aspect of life that must be horrifying to her. He looked at her and said, 'Do you want me to go on or have you had your fill for the moment?'

Suddenly they were both startled by a posse of cockatoos shrieking overhead. Even as it startled them it also served to diminish some of the tension of their discussion.

They both giggled.

'Please go on,' her gentle voice encouraged.

Quietly, he told her how the local chief of police apparently helped his parents escape Warsaw, and how he couldn't help but wonder whether the policeman had been infatuated with his mother, who was very attractive. He had never asked his mother about this, not wanting to hurt her.

'Gillian,' he went on, 'I feel that I've loaded you and myself up, with enough trauma for today. I hope you don't think I'm looking for sympathy because I'm not. But it is a bit of a safety valve emotionally to share this with someone who cares. Maybe it will help you understand and tolerate some of my ways that might otherwise appear strange. I'll explain later why I was persuaded to present myself as Lee Gold when my real name is Brian Wright. It's actually not the name I was given at birth, just the one my parents adopted when we came as refugees to Birmingham. The Customs Officer checking us in said "You'll be right mate." So our family name became Wright'.

'I was born, I was named…' He paused, unsure of whether to continue. 'No, let's leave it as Brian Wright, which is when life began for me post-nightmare.'

Brian added that he wanted Gillian to continue using the name Lee, as that was his identity at the hospital, and it had to remain that way. Again, he promised he would fully explain everything to her soon.

He then took a deep breath and shared the last of what was on his mind: 'About two months after we were helped to escape from the camp, it was demolished and everyone in it was either killed or sent to other camps where they were exterminated. My mother and I lived together in Warsaw on false papers and my father lived separate from us. I can't really imagine the horror my mother must've experienced living outside the Warsaw ghetto, where most of the Jews were trapped. And then seeing the ghetto demolished and the people in it murdered – her brothers and father included. We only have a few photos from that period, and many of those possess holes. I learned this was done to disguise the faces of other people in case we were caught.'

'I haven't got a clue why my parents lived apart after escaping the camp.'

He continued somewhat heatedly: 'All this garbage has had me thinking for many years about the nature of evil. There was probably no more educated nation in Europe than Germany at the time, yet there were doctors there willing to kill their patients, teachers willing to kill their pupils, and so on. But don't think for one moment that it was the Germans alone. I believe that nearly all the nations around the world carry some responsibility for standing by and saying nought. In fact, the first person to lodge an official complaint was an Aboriginal man in Australia who tried to submit a protest to the German Embassy in Melbourne, which they refused to take. That was William Cooper. He didn't feel a special affinity with Jews, but he could relate to people being persecuted because of their race.

Many of his family members have since kept up communications with the Jewish community, so that the history of oppression and killing is not forgotten.'

Gillian suddenly threw her arms around Brian and hugged him, for a long time, allowing them both to share the cinnamon fragrance.

Later, when they were walking back to the hospital, Brian again felt astounded at how much he had told Gillian. It was almost like a therapy session, a thought he did not share with her. As they strolled in silence, Brian was aware of his face feeling flushed and some moisture floating beneath his eyelids.

After he and Gillian had parted, he felt the urge to write a new poem, scribbling down the thoughts as they came to him. He titled it 'Born to be bullied'.

> *They pummelled my body*
> *and my spirits as well.*
> *Why is being different bad?*
> *I was different*
> *or was it them?*
> *Why did it matter?*
> *They never told me*
> *as they pummelled my body*
> *and my spirits as well.*
> *Which difference is better,*
> *how can one tell?*
> *What if I took all of you to live in Japan,*
> *who would be different then?*
> *If I took us all to Japan*
> *we would be different,*
> *both I and them,*
> *now having something in common*
> *in that faraway land.*
> *Inside, so they tell me,*
> *we are all the same,*

but they never looked inside
before pummelling me each day.
So how do you measure
which difference is better?
Is it the colour of skin
or the prayers said when we sin?
Clothing may only cover
some of the differences
between one another,
our ability to speak the same words
determined by where we live
and what we are taught.
Does the god we believe in
tell us we're the same,
made in his or her image,
and in that way we remain?
So I tried to erase,
tried to disguise the differences,
but those around me
recalled how I'd been
and wouldn't let me be free.
Differences marked the victim,
Differences determined who would be pummelled,
making them easier to find
and allowing nowhere to hide.
I tried to mask my tears
as they would be different too.
I avoided telling my parents
as their mangled English and diet from afar
marked them as one of the few.
Then there was one day in the Jewish calendar
when my parents were meant to fast,
and instead, they drank to excess
with effects that were visible and guaranteed to last.
I wish I'd been born here

and not over there.
I wish my religion
wasn't different to those who stared.
I wish my clothing
didn't come from the old land.
I wish I could hide
safe from their tongues and hands.
As I got older
and more like this or that,
how did I then treat
newcomers to this land?
I sensed their differences,
they bothered me a bit.
I fought this feeling,
hoping my children would remain sweet.
I tried to teach them
that inside we're the same
and should be able and free
to choose how we dress and pray.
So, I hope they see
that being different is not bad.
As I tell them how I heard
what a wise man said.
If you cut me, I bleed,
and so do you all,
no matter the differences,
no matter what you say.
I've gradually grown to accept
many of my differences
that others won't respect,
or am I just pretending
and haven't really done that?
My aim is to be able to see
all the variations and differences
and have them no longer

able to offend or to scare what is me.
I don't flaunt my differences
nor pretend they are better,
but I don't need to hide them
nor feel them inferior,
no longer wishing to be safe
from their hostile tongues and hands.
I didn't choose my religion,
it chose me at birth,
and I have no intention
of letting it submerge.
I believe all religions
should be about only one thing,
treating each other
the way we want to be treated ourselves.
I have no wish for revenge,
but actually, I do.
So, I bury it fast,
believing the saying 'An eye for an eye',
and the whole world goes blind.
Well, I am not really a poet
but the message is true
and should only bother the pedantic few.

Chapter 17

Not so long ago, Brian had been left shattered by the letter Penny had sent him, ending their relationship. At the time, he'd wondered if there would ever be any newfound happiness in his life. Now, he'd begun to believe it was possible that someone like Gillian, with everything she had to offer, might want to be with him.

But questions continued to nag at him: weren't other guys lining up to be with her? And wouldn't she be tempted by one of them?

To Brian's amazement, he extracted from deep within himself the courage to ask Gillian that very question. They had finished work for the day and were sitting in the small lounge adjacent to his bedroom, in the modest apartment he rented. He sensed the sweat ebbing from his body along with all his courage, and before the latter vanished, he forced the words out.

In response, Gillian gently confirmed there were many guys who were interested in her, and that she had made it clear there could only be friendship between her and them, nothing more than that.

She then reminded Brian that she had never imposed that limit on him.

Brian felt blessed as he gazed at Gillian's blonde locks and sparkling eyes and imbibed the warmth of her smile and words.

Not long after this conversation, Brian and Gillian returned to their private spot on the flat rocks, and this time it was Gillian's turn to share her innermost story. She described how she had been married once, revealing a pent-up sadness under the jolly facade she presented to the outside world most of the time.

Gillian said her husband was an introvert and that various traumas in his earlier life had flattened his personality and drive, as if he had been run over by a cement mixer. Despite that, she had wanted to marry him, as she felt he possessed a strong warmth and kindness. However, no amount of support and love from her was sufficient to keep his depression at bay, and she could only watch as he experienced deeper and deeper bouts of despair, which eventually took his life. Gillian said that for a while she blamed herself for not having prevented the tragedy, but with the help of a psychologist she began seeing it more accurately and she eventually stopped beating herself up. An inner voice spoke up very quietly: 'I know deep down that I could and should have done more to prevent that tragedy. At the time I was fearful of intruding. I know for sure now that I should have intruded.'

Brian hugged her, feeling her moist cheek against his face.

The life history just flowed from Gillian, despite the emotions it aroused, still quite raw.

She obviously had a need to share it with Brian. He thought to himself that she might well have imagined she could be a therapist for her husband, bringing about the necessary change in him, only to realise that role was not hers to play and that possibly she didn't play it well.

Then he couldn't help wondering if there was any human being who was totally free from disturbance and trauma in their life.

As Gillian spoke about her husband, a shadow of a smile flitted across Brian's face. He hoped Gillian hadn't noticed it, because if she asked what that look meant, he knew he couldn't answer truthfully.

What went through his mind had been the thought—she really picks losers—that the two men who loved her could not make a go of things.

He realised that she had seen the worth in the man her late husband had been and maybe convinced herself she could get him right.

He realised his private thought was cruel and mainly a dig at himself. He was determined that rather than her being his therapist he'd work on himself and even maybe see a professional therapist.

He hugged Gill yet again (as he'd begun to call her) and promised himself that whatever it took to fully realise this relationship with Gill, he'd make it happen. The reality part of him frowned, acknowledging there were many hurdles to still clear and sort out. This included his present criminal activities. He believed he was a good therapist but acknowledged to himself that he had no legal right to do it in this manner.

There were a lot of caves to search before he found the right path, he knew, and shared it with himself.

Brian came to recognise the sensitivity Gillian displayed when she was with the patients under her care. It also became apparent that she felt, like him, that there should be a tolerance of people's differences. They both agreed that being eccentric shouldn't lead to bullying or hospitalisation. This attitude on Gillian's part was most obvious when she and Brian mixed with a nurse called Violet, whose social downfall was her apparent lack of interest in what other people thought or said. Lee noticed that if someone else was talking and paused to take a breath, Violet would jump in and capture the focus for herself. But Gillian was loyal to Violet, refusing to exclude her company, and Brian found this admirable.

One evening, as they lay together on Brian's sofa, he decided to share with Gillian a poem that described the way he felt before he met her. However, he did not wish to scare her, given her experience with her former husband, and began by reassuring her that the words did not represent what he was going through now, nor did they mean he wasn't coping with his emotions. Rather, he was confronting what he strongly felt and sharing it with someone he cared about deeply.

The world makes no sense to him,
he can't understand
why people continue to hate him
in every piece of land.
The rules of the world
don't apply to him, you can be sure,
but he is surrounded by people
who want him gone and even more.
These are the same people
who profess to seek peace,
yet they're not the rules they apply:
for anyone who succeeds.
The more he succeeds
the more he is hated.
If he'd only roll over
then I'm sure he would be feted.

Brian gently took Gillian into his arms. 'I'm not sure why this has come into my head. Maybe it's because things are going so well, I am petrified someone will try and destroy it.'

Then he told Gillian he had another piece he wanted to read to her, on evil. 'Bet you've never heard an evil poem before,' said Brian with a smile, eliciting a nervous grin from Gillian.

What is evil, you may well ask.
To define and predict it becomes quite a task.

I ponder whether evil is so widespread,
yet I know deep down that I believe,
we can all be led in varying degrees.
None of us can be sure that we are totally free
of the underlying rage and urges
that can readily harm you and me.
Life experiences can mould us poorly or well,
so, as I age I begin myself to tell
that evil is what evil does,
it corrupts and hurts the perpetrator
and the spectator as well,
who can both end up going to Hell.
Many of my friends are now ailing or dead
and when we congregate, many organ recitals are said
conducted and led by those still alive
who have concern and anxiety filling their head.
But just remember evil is sin
Brought on not only by those that do it
But equally by the spectator who stands and grins.
So what do I measure at this stage of life,
wondering if it's preferable to live meaningfully
or merely survive.

Brian took stock of what he'd just recited. 'I can't believe what a dill I am. Not having been this happy for a very, very long time. If ever. I guess I am terrified of losing that happiness, so I'm drowning it in fear and negative thoughts. Gillian, if I start going off on a tangent like this in the future, just whack me on the head and stop me.'

Gillian promised she would. But even before she'd finished affirming this, Brian was already introducing another twist into their conversation: 'Some of what I've written in my poems reflects my belief that one thing that possibly drives people towards religion is fear of the unknown. In some ways, it feels safer to believe there is a higher being regulating what happens in our lives, rather than the idea that what occurs in our lives is largely governed by chance, by us and the roll of the dice. I've just started trying to write a poem about this called *The Passage of Life*.'

I am tired of hiding a bit of myself,
I am tired of lying,
pretending to always be well,
tired of appearing to be someone other than myself.
I began by hiding that I was a Jew,
then I pretended to be a true blood through and through,
but to do that I hid who my parents were.
I have no memory for some years gone by
which enabled me to hide and eventually survive.
As well as all the gaps in my memory long past,
I've lost so many close to me
where no memory lasts.
I cannot recall them nor have photos to see.
I don't know where their bodies are buried
or whether they have been cast to the sea.
Some of what I do remember
I gladly put aside
as they were painful years,
seeking where we could safely hide and survive.
There are no graves of relatives to pay respect,
no photos to remind me that I can inspect.
The photos could give me a sense of the past,
for without a past and a future,
very little of significance may be able to last.
I do have a few photos,
mainly with holes here and there,
stripping their identity glaringly bare.
I collect photos obsessively
as they connect me with present and past.
Without these connections

one cannot have a lifeline that continues to last.
For this was their wish,
to make both me and my race extinct,
so it could only be remembered in a museum
like the dodo or a sphinx.
Now a final word
that needs to be said
about all those who only stood and observed,
watching us become dead.
I believe they are equally responsible
for the millions who disappeared
once life ceased and they became dead.
The perpetrators and audience
Are both to blame
One free to carry out the evil
Whilst the other allows the green light to shine.

Chapter 18

Brian felt more and more that he was settling into a lifestyle that he had been seeking for a long time. For the first time, people were seeing him as the person he was, rather than being influenced by his family of origin. However, the sour taste of fear occasionally slipped onto his tongue, for it was still the reality that he continued to live a life that was partly a lie. He reassured himself by thinking about a study that claimed most Americans believed professional wrestling was real, but the moon landing was a fake.

In two days' time, Brian was due to attend a conference on psychiatric disorders in Sydney, as was Gillian. To help relax themselves beforehand, the pair arranged to go out for dinner in Katherine on their own rather than with friends, to give themselves the chance to talk without having to play any particular role.

They went to a nearby wine bar, Manny's, with Brian surprised by how trendy it appeared. There were only a few diners there, still being somewhat early in the evening, but the place did appear inviting and fresh. The only thing that seemed to be missing were staff, as Brian could not find anyone to take their order. Then a gaunt young man emerged through the swinging doors that separated the dining area from the kitchen. His head was shaven, and he had two rings in his ears. In silence, this waiter thrust a menu towards Brian and Gillian, and proceeded to recite the specials of the day from a nearby chalkboard before abruptly striding off.

Brian could not help but think back to a line he'd once heard, perhaps from the Marx Brothers or Woody Allen, who'd said if a meal was so special, then why not print it on the menu. He doubted this waiter would be amused.

They eventually ordered by pointing either to the menu or to the board, Brian amazed at how little need there was for language in this situation, and how little interest the waiter appeared to have in them. They ate rapidly and were finished in just over an hour or so, which struck Brian as very different to the rest of his life, where he tried to slow things down to stay on top of them. He left what he felt was a somewhat exorbitant tip, before noticing other customers coming into the restaurant and the waiter treating them in a very different manner, beaming a smile and interacting.

At this point, Brian thought to himself that he should probably rein in the amount of thinking that he did when he was with other people. If he did not, it might well create a barrier to him interacting with others, as he became immersed and drowning in his own thoughts, lost in preoccupation.

After dinner, he dropped Gillian off at her apartment and popped into the hospital, where he needed to sign some paperwork to do with his wages. The secretary in the superintendent's office, Rosie, was a friendly, chirpy lady who was working late. Brian recalled how, when he was studying in Birmingham, another medical resident had told Brian what he felt was the secret to employing a good secretary. He said one needed to look for a middle-aged lady who was either single or separated, preferably without children or children who had left home. It would help, according to this resident, if the lady happened to be someone physically plain and who did not have much of a social life, with few outside interests. At the time, Brian felt the description was particularly cruel and insensitive, but he had to admit to himself now that it seemed to fit Rosie. From what he knew of her, she wanted to give to people, but at home had no-one to give to. Thus, she appeared to be married to her job, with all her generosity coming out in the work environment.

O

Brian couldn't recall the last time he'd been invited to a formal dinner party, and this one, on the night before the psychiatric conference was due to start, was quite the affair. Given Brian hadn't gone to many parties, and this one was taking place in Sydney amongst a lot of people he'd never met before, it left him feeling a high degree of anxiety and self-doubt, even with the improvements in his own confidence lately. Yet these negative feelings were tinged with a degree of pleasure at being drawn into the crowd.

The blonde lady sitting on his left was just one stranger among the many around him, but she was someone most people couldn't avoid noticing.

She made sure of that.

Brian felt that some of her features may have been enhanced by surgical manoeuvres. The glowing flesh beyond the tight, low-cut blouse was hard to miss, as were her over-endowed lips. Not for the first time when seeing a woman presenting in this manner, Brian wondered whether she was doing it purely for herself, or to have other women look at her, or for male attention. Or could it be all of the above. Whatever her motivation, he found her eyes moving in his direction more than he expected or felt comfortable with, for her gaze didn't waver if he happened to catch her looking. A slight smile lit her eyes and the rest of her face.

Brian glanced over to where Gillian had been seated, further down the long table and on the other side from him. It puzzled him why they weren't sitting closer to each other, though he suspected the organisers of the dinner may have felt the attendees, who were from all over the country - some from overseas - would mix more that way. Gillian and he caught each other's eyes and both smiled, acknowledging the seductive behaviour Brian was exposed to, and giving him a tick for remaining on an even keel.

Without doubt the diner next to him was sexy, the plunging neckline hard to ignore, but there was no way he was going to threaten his developing relationship with Gillian. Still, there was some pleasure in having other people notice her interest in him.

Not for the first time, Brian found himself wondering what it was about the female breast that men found so fascinating. It must be more complex than the flippant theory of it being related to the trauma of having to give up the breast and go on the bottle.

Suddenly he felt a hand resting on his thigh. He decided he would not make a fuss. Why not enjoy the moment if it went no further? Was this really the mixing the organisers of the party had in mind? He smiled to himself at that notion.

Having glanced at the name card placed on the table in front of his curvaceous neighbour, Brian said the obvious: 'Phoebe, isn't it?'

A sharp pinch of his thigh confirmed that he was correct. Brian then noticed a man staring at him from further along the table, continuing to do so even when Brian caught him doing it.

'Phoebe,' he said to the woman beside him, 'you're married, aren't you? What's his name?'

'It's Ralph. That's him over there. He's probably looking this way because he doesn't like me talking to other men.'

O

Syntology's headquarters had been thrilled at hearing the news that Ralph brought them – a wonderful piece of evidence for revealing the incompetence of psychiatry and the harm it caused to so many in society. They chose not to rush publicising the Riverdale experiment, however, as the longer it continued undetected, the more it highlighted the incompetence of psychiatry and those who practised it.

Ralph, meanwhile, had set about trying to locate where Brian, or Jerome, had fled. The police had tried to follow his trail but without immediate success, so they had let it go, suspecting he had altered his name once again. After some pressure from Syntology, they pursued the idea of seeing whether any airline personnel could visually identify Brian from photographs shown to them. Nothing happened for several weeks, then Ralph took a phone call at his apartment.

'Look, I won't give you my name because I shouldn't give out private information and it hasn't been subpoenaed,' said the caller. 'So, off the record, this man you're looking for, he caught a flight to Melbourne, Australia a few weeks back under name of Lee Gold.' The person then hurriedly hung up, with an audible click.

Ralph had recently begun working for a medical equipment firm as a salesman, but now he took a fortnight off – an act smoothed by Syntology people connected with the company. He then checked what medical conferences were on in Australia in the near future, and discovered to his delight that one on psychiatric disorders was due to begin in Sydney in a couple of weeks. Again, with the help of Syntology contacts, he was able to access the conference guest list, whereupon he found that a Dr. Lee Gold had recently registered for it. Ralph booked himself and Phoebe into a hotel adjacent to where the conference was being held, and where it appeared the other delegates were staying.

The top brass in Syntology had developed a theory, seconded by Ralph, that for Brian to rapidly gain approval to practise or have some level of involvement in psychiatry, pointed to the likelihood that he was now based in a small town. They suspected that this type of situation could generate an offer of some kind on the part of a regional hospital without careful screening of the applicant's paperwork, given how desperate they often were in finding staff.

With their extensive contacts, Syntology had little difficulty drawing up a short list of places to investigate.

By now Syntology were aware of the quandary that Carlos, who was connected with their group, found himself in. They communicated with Carlos, reassuring him they would help him get out of gaol, but felt if he stayed a bit longer it would reflect badly on Brian for not helping him.

O

The day after the dinner, on the first day of the conference proper, Brian sat listening to a somewhat soporific lecture on the difference between infatuation and true love. He'd noticed quite early on that Ralph, whom he now knew by sight, was sitting a couple of rows in front and to the right of him. Ralph frequently turned around to smile at him, or maybe it was more of a smirk. Either way, Brian felt sure that ill will was being communicated toward him.

That evening, a cocktail party was held after dinner for the people attending the conference. The room was cleared of tables and place settings. Brian and Gillian were standing talking to each other when Ralph suddenly intruded, his voice piercing the calm. 'I thought I should introduce myself,' he droned. 'I am the son of the late Dr. Klein.'

The sneer took hold of Ralph's smile distorting the layout of his lips.

Brian, not one hundred per cent sure if he was dealing with friend or foe, and surprised by this turn of events, began to offer condolences, but was abruptly cut short by Ralph.

'I thought I should share with you a recent experience. I was going through my father's papers' – especially the will, thought Brian – 'and guess what I found there? I discovered that he'd involved you in an experiment where you were admitted to Riverdale as a patient in one of its wards. Amazing that none of the staff realised you weren't ill. So, I heard that you then had to escape from the ward, because they thought you were seriously ill. You then took on a new name and falsified records and got a job as a clinical psychiatrist even though you have not trained in that field yet. I also heard that a staff member in Riverdale, nursing aide Carlos, was jailed, with police thinking that he had done away with you. I imagine you knew that he was jailed, so I wonder why you did not help him out.'

Brian stared at Ralph in disbelief, stung by the venom that Ralph's words were conveying. The deep shadow of Ralph's sneer darkened the space between them.

'I guess I should let you know,' continued Ralph, 'that I belong to a group you might be familiar with, called Syntology. Now the Church of Syntology has strong feelings about the way psychiatry is practised, and you may find those feelings begin to be expressed in the media in the coming days.' Without pausing for breath, and with a smirk that refused to go away, Ralph then fired the next shot: 'I wonder what the medical board is going to think of you practising as a psychiatrist without having trained as one. Make sure you start reading the papers from tomorrow.'

Ralph's capacity for malice appeared to have no bounds, and with his sheer meanness of spirit distorting his face, he walked off, leaving Brian with a multitude of thoughts dashing around his head - very few of them pleasant. Gillian put her hand on his back, sensing his distress but confused as to what had just gone on. She gave him a hug, seeing that he was close to tears.

'Gill,' he told her, 'I need to let you know I love you and I'm ashamed about not being totally open with you in the past. I think I didn't want to hurt you, but even more than that, I didn't want you to think less of me.'

They continued hugging each other. Enclosed in a wall of tears, Lee, who had now become Brian with Gillian, attempted to help her understand the catastrophe now engulfing him.

Brian barely slept that night. The next morning, he went in search of a daily paper and soon found one in the hotel lobby. On the front page was the headline "*One man's normality converts to a psychiatrist's psychosis*", followed by text that named him. Saying little to each other or anyone else, Brian and Gill cut short their attendance at the conference and headed back to Katherine as quickly as they could.

O

Over the next few days, the national media carried a range of headlines about the Riverdale experiment, either on the front page or close to it:

TOTALLY HEALTHY DOCTOR PATIENT VIEWED AS PSYCHOTIC BY PSYCHIATRISTS.

HOW MANY HEALTHY PEOPLE ARE MISDIAGNOSED AND TREATED BY PSYCHIATRISTS?

THE GAME OF PSYCHIATRY – A PRECISE SCIENCE?

THE WAY PSYCHIATRY FUNCTIONS, IT CAN NEVER RUN OUT OF PATIENTS.

The barrage continued in an unrelenting manner, each headline leading into a graphic description of the incompetence of psychiatry and how the alleged profession would stoop to doing anything to accumulate patients. Brian found that his colleagues in Katherine kept a safe distance at this time, with one exception, besides Gill.

He struggled to not feel as if he was a criminal who had just been exposed. However, the truth he had to face was that he had committed a criminal act in pretending to be a trained psychiatrist. The only comforting thought was the knowledge that he had done his utmost to provide his patients with proper care, and as far as he knew, no patient of his had suffered from his care.

A psychiatrist called Dr. Alexander Jonas had, in a short space of time, put a lot of work into understanding what was going on, and he had decided that in many ways psychiatry had let Brian down. He was aware that the way Brian had dealt with the situation lay outside the rules and was unethical. However, Dr. Jonas also acknowledged how much effort Lee had put into treating the patients under his care in a competent manner, and how he had done so much to educate himself.

Dr. Jonas had met Lee several times when Lee was caring for patients referred by. Dr. Jonas. Quite a few of the nursing staff were also supportive of Brian, impressed by the quality of care he was demonstrating with patients, and the patients themselves also appeared to think highly of him.

And yet the media attacks continued, with Brian struggling to stay afloat. With the daily public exposures and accusations he found himself measuring the reactions of people he knew towards him. He noted many young doctors who he knew only superficially were keeping their distance for fear they could be caught up in the accusations. The irony of the situation hit him, as he realised that the pressure he was facing could well drag him down to the point where he needed psychiatric care himself. If that happened, he would have gone from being in a psychiatric ward and not requiring treatment but getting it, to someone who now genuinely needed treatment.

The image of Ralph with a smirk, wishing him harm, flashed in his mind as Brian obsessively thought about Ralph's role in sparking these attacks. It also occurred to him that Ralph, once he discovered the research that had been set up by his father, could have done something to help him, and could have helped Carlos as well. But he had chosen not to, exploiting the situation to provide his sect with an opportunity to strike at the heart of psychiatry, and in the process demolish Brian.

Brian fantasised about getting revenge on Ralph, while warning himself with the saying of how an obsession with revenge means digging two graves. He could sense the potential for self-harm.

Inevitably, someone must have leaked Brian's address to the press, as they set up camp outside his apartment block. He knew that he would have to move as soon as possible, in the most anonymous way, but where do you hide in a small town.

The headlines continued:

How to Differentiate a Healthy Person From One Who is Severely Ill – The First Step is to Not Ask a Psychiatrist.

What Training Do You Need to be a Psychiatrist? – None, Because Psychiatry is Not Based on Knowledge.

Psychiatry can be Practiced Without Training--as Some do at Present.

The media continued to describe how the staff at Riverdale had not been able to detect that Jerome was well, instead just accepting what was written in his file. They also described how he got his job as a psychiatrist with papers that had been falsified, which had not been detected during the application process nor when he began working.

Throughout this turmoil, a recurring wish assaulted Brian's mind, nestling in the cloud of fury inside his head. It was a wish to get revenge by inflicting pain on Ralph.

Gillian continued to be supportive, though Lee struggled to believe that her support would last and not be eroded. Surprisingly, though, he realised that for the first time in his life he was not living a lie, that what he was saying was totally true, just extremely pressured. And in his better moments, he had to acknowledge to himself, and to Gill, that it had been wrong to falsify papers saying he had trained as a psychiatrist. And that it had been wrong to allow Carlos to rot in prison because he feared that to help the orderly would expose his own subterfuge.

But Brian found that the other staff, apart from Dr. Jonas, continued to stay away from him – in fact, they increased the gap as much as they could. He understood their fear of being caught up in the mess that was going on, and possibly the fear of receiving criticism for not having detected that Brian had fraudulently presented as a fully trained psychiatrist.

Brian attempted to console himself, reflecting that even though he was guilty of a terrible ruse, he believed he had kept his patients' interests as his prime objective. He felt this contrasted with the Syntology sect's aim of wanting to achieve some sort of control by exploiting patients and demolishing the competitors they identified in psychiatry. He was not aware of having hurt or damaged anyone that he treated, but rather experienced joy from how his former patients rang and left him positive messages or wrote appreciative notes. He had to think of them as *former* patients because he had ceased work until all these issues could be sorted out.

Nonetheless, it was getting increasingly difficult for Brian to keep his growing anxiety and depression at bay. He had believed for a long time that many of the patients he was seeing had been hurt or damaged by other people, and that people hurting people was a common theme in many psychiatric disorders – if not most of them. He also believed that the opposite of love was indifference. People standing by during the Holocaust while an attempt was made to wipe out an entire race, that was chilling to contemplate. Very few people had attempted to stop what was going on.

He knew that it was easy to be numbed by the enormous number of people who were murdered, not to mention the unrealised lives of the children and grandchildren who would have been born had the murders not occurred. But in contrast to the bystanders who did nothing during the period of those atrocities, there were a few designated as righteous who had risked everything to help another human being.

He realised that many factors could lead to being a bystander. It could be out of fear, or a wish to gain in some way, be it a job or property. Or it might reflect the bystander carrying the same prejudice as those committing the atrocities. Not for the first time, he found himself reflecting on humanity's potential for good, but possibly its greater potential for harm and malice, wondering whether the capacity for malice lay stored in every human being, including himself. He knew he had hurt people over the years, knowingly at times, but he shuddered at the thought that he could do worse than that.

When he did a rough count of people he had let down, quite a few significant names came to mind in a bitter stream. They included his mother, Jill, Carlos, Tom and possibly Penny. There were also nameless individuals such as women he had slept with for his own sexual gratification before moving on and dropping any further contact with them. People let people down all the time and hurt them in various ways.

He also felt increasing hurt by the way doctors he knew from his work were now avoiding him as much as they could, as if any contact could contaminate them. It had been a while since he last saw Roger, but Brian met up with him as he emerged from a local supermarket and was confronted by the painful vision of Roger's grinning smirk. He was sure Roger had sought him out, the man's manner and words confirming this was no chance meeting. 'Well, well, well,' said Roger, 'you've really hijacked the news. Every time I open a newspaper or turn on the radio, there you are. You might recall I warned you about the approach you were adopting with patients. It makes sense now. You hadn't had any training.'

Brian controlled his urge to respond to the bitter bullets fired at him and strode off.

Chapter 19

Brian managed to hold back from seeking revenge, but he gave himself the freedom to express it in fantasies and dreams, and in his writing.

There was a cartoonist for a daily paper, *The Agarol*, who Brian fiercely resented, and had done so for quite a while, well before his current problems.

The man had in the past been accused of being a Holocaust denier. When the attacks commenced at the instigation of Syntology, using the vehicle of the media, Brian found himself increasingly mocked by a cartoonist, who went by the name of Schreiber. So, he expressed his bitterness in a short poem, 'An ode to Schreiber,' which was not sent to any media organisation nor to the cartoonist himself, but which still provided an emotional outlet for Brian's rage.

Blindness and bias tend to create the image of liars.
Schreiber is false to himself and those he inspires.

> *It's easy in comfort to pontificate aloud,*
> *in the safety of ignorance, with head in the cloud.*
> *There are times when turning the other cheek,*
> *and being humble and forgiving and a little meek,*
> *are merely covers for the crimes of mass evil*
> *such as Holocaust denial, as Neville Chamberlain could confirm if*
> *he was still living.*
> *Whilst Schreiber continues his sordid dreaming, content with*
> *his lot,*
> *let him explain his ideas to past victims of Hitler and more*
> *recently Pol Pot.*

Brian also jotted down a skewed take on a well-known verse.

> *Mirror, mirror on the wall,*
> *I hate McDonald's and poppies tall.*
> *Show me only what I want to see*
> *and for my drivel, pay me a weekly fee.*
> *Demonstrate to my detractors my firm belief*
> *that it's the victim who is at fault, and not the rapist or the thief.*

Brian was consumed with tension, avoiding people. If he could not manage that he monitored their reactions, wondering what they were thinking. He would find himself looking into their eyes to see what he could read about their reactions toward him. The only person he felt entirely safe with was Gillian, and she remained extremely supportive, though the doubt lay in him that she might not continue to tolerate this pressure or could even begin to mistrust him.

He preferred to go out at night, when he was less likely to be recognised, but Gillian encouraged him to go out during the day with her when she was not working. One day, Gill encouraged Brian to go on a double date that night, where he and Gillian would be joined by a young orthopaedic surgeon and his girlfriend. Although Brian found himself almost constantly on edge these days, he had to admit that it was a pleasant evening, where he felt able to put his concerns aside. They ate at a restaurant that Gillian loved, where the staff obviously knew and liked her, and throughout the night there was no mention of anything that alluded to Brian's current problems.

Later, he drove Gillian home, and before she exited the car they shared a few moments of intimacy. Gillian had an early-morning shift, so she caressed Brian's face and then kissed him good night, arranging that they would speak the next day, probably in the evening.

As Brian drove slowly back towards his apartment, trying to hold on to the warmth of the evening, he was suddenly enveloped by a cacophony of rough automobile sounds, sounds that did not belong to a vehicle if it had been serviced adequately. In his rear-view mirror, he glimpsed a large car travelling at excessive speed. As it got closer, Brian realised with a jolt that it was making no attempt to avoid a collision. Then there was a jarring clunk and the other vehicle came up alongside him. It was occupied by three grinning faces, young men who were probably all close to 20 years of age. They appeared to be muscular, and overly happy about the collision. One of them yelled out some nonsense along the lines that Brian should have been travelling faster, and the car then sped off, the driver tooting its horn.

At that stage, it did not penetrate Brian's mind that Syntology members came in all shapes and sizes. Whilst it is said that suspicion crowds the vessel in which it resides, his vessel would remain empty for the remainder of the night. He stopped his car to check the damage, thinking he could probably get it fixed for not too much money. After some more thought, he decided there was no point in reporting the incident to the police, as he had enough on his plate already.

The following day he found in his letterbox an anonymous note stating that the crash was the penalty for his sins. Accompanying this note was another which was only semi-anonymous, as it identified as originating from the offices of Syntology. This note went on to say that the previous night, sect members had come together and recited the mantra: *'To Dr. Lee Gold we bequeath this curse. May he forever return to dust and earth.'*

Brian stood there in shock for several minutes, not ready to focus or think about anything, feeling only fear about what might happen next. He was deeply troubled by the capacity some showed for cruelty.

Brian wished he could put aside the incident, and stop being consumed by his doubts, but with Syntology mocking and destroying his reputation, and that of psychiatry as well, those doubts had become overwhelming.

It struck him how ironic the situation had become. On the one hand he was praying for a time when the attacks on his own integrity and that of psychiatry would cease, yet not so long ago he had found himself bitterly grieving the memories he had lost, or which had been taken from him. It felt like the early part of his life had been erased, as had many of the people in those memories: grandparents, uncles, aunts. What scraps of remembering he could retrieve, he hung onto desperately.

He strongly believed that whether memories were sweet or bitter, they remained essential, for without them one did not have a past, nor perhaps a future – it would be like being a vegetable or suspended in time. He had started reflecting that his somewhat obsessive hoarding of photographs in times, was his attempt to connect the pieces of his life and desperately hang onto them.

He began to think about the whole question of sects, cults and religion. He had read that there was some similarity between all the faiths, and he was starting to believe that might be the case. He certainly agreed with some, that the more extreme religious groups had a degree of overlap with Syntology. Some of them demanded money from their followers, or there was an element of strict obedience, or sometimes the threat of punishment, and varying degrees of exploitation. The more standard religious groups had a better profile, but even with them he felt there was the implied threat of a penalty from God if one did not follow the rules that had been laid out.

○

It was now approaching two months since Brian's life had blown up. Brian was making an even bigger effort to include Gillian in many of the thoughts going through his mind, which was a new experience for him.

In the past, the person he spoke to the most had been himself. But there had been mention in the media recently about police involvement in his case, and Brian had no doubt that things were going to get even worse and be more publicised, inevitably leading to his deregistration – even if the hospital had not terminated Brian's employment for the time being. As far as he could tell, all of this was leading to just one thing.

Under the relentless bombardment from Syntology, Brian had to acknowledge to himself that the level of anxiety and depression he was carrying warranted treatment by a psychiatrist, and he further hoped that acting promptly to get the help he required would assist him in avoiding being hospitalised.

Though Gillian had reassured him about her love and wanting to have a permanent relationship, it did not prevent insecurity and fear creeping in and eroding Brian's security about their relationship. Time and again, he punished himself with the thought that Gillian had tried to hang on and save one partner she loved, and then had to cope with the traumatic loss of him suiciding. How could she risk subjecting herself to loving another man with severe depression?

That evening they sat in the garden quietly having a drink when suddenly Brian felt overwhelmed with a deep sadness that he couldn't hide, as his voice broke, and tears streamed down his cheeks.

Gillian drew him to her and quietly hugged him. 'Do you want to tell me about it?' she asked gently.

'I'm scared to but I will.' He spoke rapidly to get the words out before his anxiety stopped the words coming.

With his moist face against her soft cheek, he whispered, 'You've lost one man. How can I expect you to risk going through that trauma again?'

Her warm, gentle gaze held him quietly at first and as she kissed him, she said in a firm voice, 'There's a saying Brian – we're all in the gutter at times but some are looking at the stars. I have always felt I could have done more with my husband to help him. It may or may not have succeeded, but I'm there for you. Please believe and trust me.'

So, Brian commenced seeing Dr. Jonas, trying to believe Gill's promise and with this support he came to a decision. It had been apparent weeks beforehand, but it was only now that he was prepared to carry it out. The decision was his alone, but the risk involved in acting on it was softened by having someone of the quality of Dr. Jonas alongside him.

He sat with Gillian one evening in the garden that surrounded her apartment block and told her that he planned to deregister himself. He explained that otherwise the whole mess would drag on, causing immeasurable damage. By doing this, he hoped it would gradually take the steam out of the whole campaign to smear his name and that of psychiatry.

'Gill, I know it won't be easy,' he said, 'but what I hope is that it puts a stop to the circus that is going on at present. Either way I will be deregistered, whether it feels fair or not.

'I can accept that there is a need for me to be penalised, to send a message to others that it is not acceptable to do some of the things that I did, even though I could see no other way. I believe I was good to my patients. I was willing to learn and ask advice, and best of all I listened to those in my care, letting them talk. I treated them as real people, real human beings who needed help with the problems they were going through. Now I know that scenario will not seem as if it offers you a lot, but I would love for you to be my partner and for us to support each other.'

Gillian did not respond in words but instead threw her arms around Brian's neck, their bodies merging in solace. Brian could feel tears starting to well up in his eyes, as they were in Gill's.

They were now facing each other, still holding on. Brian said: 'Do you want to think about it? What I'm asking is that we share our lives together, and that's not going to be easy, as you've seen.'

Before Brian could say anything else, Gillian put her finger on his lips. 'Shush. There is nothing I want more than for us to be together in the future.'

But Brian had more to say. 'I've been thinking a lot about our life together, and again, it won't be easy, because for the first time in my life I feel like people can see the real me. I won't be judged by my parents or any other factors. What you see and relate to is what you get. I am going to attempt to change myself in a whole lot of ways.'

As he wiped his eyes, he reflected on an old Chinese saying: '*Before we can see properly, we must shed our tears to clear the way*. I believe that I can use the skills that I have acquired, to help disadvantaged people, maybe people in Third World countries. And I feel I could be useful as a counsellor for people caught up in drugs or under the influence of sects like Syntology. I might have to get a job as a labourer to provide some more money for us to live on in the early days. It all sounds simple, though I assure you it won't be. But I've already sent a letter to the patients previously under my care, so they don't feel rejected and cast aside.'

Making the decision to deregister himself took some of the weight off Brian's shoulders, and from Gillian's too. Later that day, Brian packed his possessions, which were few, and moved in with Gill. He felt happy within himself, though there was a long way to go. Whilst he had the courage and the will, he lined up an appointment to tell the hospital authorities about his choice. He also began looking around to find help groups that he could become involved with, especially in disadvantaged parts of the local community. He knew the media and Syntology would not readily forgive him for taking the air out of their sails, and that they had considerable resources – especially Syntology, which would forever see him as a target.

However, over the next five or so weeks, the attacks gradually diminished, but he knew it didn't come with guarantees. He imagined from what he'd learnt about Syntology, that it could be the lull before yet another storm. He imagined with a degree of anxiety that the sect could be constructing new rounds of ammunition. He told Gill what he thought and feared to some degree, he told his patients what he was planning so they didn't feel deserted. Most of all, he told himself, hoping it would help him be prepared for any attack launched.

The next night, before going to bed, he and Gill sat quietly on a bench in the cool air, beside the accommodation they were now sharing. They had become comfortable with each other's silences, if there was nothing to say. Then Gill turned to Brian and said, 'I hope you don't mind me reading some of the stuff you leave lying around. I came across a little piece called *The Search for Meaning* and it was different but really cute. Are you able to tell me a bit more about it?'

'Well,' replied Brian, 'you know how I feel about having some purpose and meaning in my life, and how I've been troubled that people rarely saw me for myself but judged me by my family or by something else. I've been wanting to feel significant in life in some way for a long time. In a quirky moment, I wrote this little piece about a sperm who wants to amount to something and be significant, not just a stain on someone's sheets. What becomes of him depends so much on the person he is in, whether he gets to meet an ovum, and whether together they can fertilise a human being. An alternative outcome could be that the sperm fails to meet an ovum, or is ejaculated and wasted.'

Gillian gave him a kiss and said, 'Why don't you publish a little bit of the story, as it has meaning at so many different levels?'

Brian laughed. 'Okay, we could even make it a children's book.'

By the following evening, he had put together a smaller version of the narrative.

'I'm tired of being underrated and wasted and anonymous too.

'Often, I end up just being a stain on a bed sheet,

or I may have been rendered impotent by spermicidal jelly.

'It hasn't been up to me which ova I meet.

'They can disregard me and see me as insignificant, just one of many.

'I decided it was time to act to realise my potential …'

So this sperm became proactive. The young man, Peter, who the sperm was housed in was rather shy. So the sperm did some research and found an attractive young woman was employed at the same place as Peter.

From his vantage point, this sperm had become aware that Peter was attracted to Leoni, that he was getting an erection when she was nearby. So he gathered the million or so other sperm in his vicinity and spread the message by what he called a 'ripple effect'.

The next time the young woman was in the vicinity, wave after wave of sperm moved forward, creating a similar effect to arousal in Peter. This, plus the impact of Peter's brain, were now primed. There was now a chance the sperm could meet a suitable ovum and something significant could emanate from that.

As the sperm liked to say, he had the potential to contribute to half an Einstein, half a Hitler, or just be a stain on the sheets. But he had done as much as he could to influence the likelihood of success.

Brian showed the story to Gillian and said, 'Okay, how about you polish it up and you can read it as a nursery rhyme to our – can I say – first child?'

Gillian and he then fell asleep in each other's arms.

Chapter 20

Whilst Brian was now feeling a lot better, and had started to be much calmer, there was still enormous pressure on him. Thus, there were still bad flare-ups at times.

One morning he listened to a message that had been left on his phone by Ralph, who wanted to make a deal of some kind, though he did not spell out anything specific. Ralph also taunted him about the damage he had caused to psychiatry and how he had successfully diminished people's confidence in it. It pushed Brian into deciding that he would get his phone number changed as soon as possible.

Brian had no intention of sharing with Ralph the information that he had effectively left psychiatry and medicine, and was planning to develop a career counselling people who were disadvantaged in one way or another. He thought to himself that what he should say to Ralph was: 'You work for an organisation that aims to control and exploit, and whilst I may be far from perfect, my aim is to listen, to help and to support.'

Brian decided he would not give the appearance of slinking away battered and bruised. As uncomfortable as it felt, he planned to meet with a range of people he had come to know through work, feeling he owed them the courtesy of explaining face to face why he was leaving.

Later that afternoon he drove for a few hours to a small settlement well outside Katherine and checked into a humble motel there, having arranged a breakfast meeting the following morning with two local doctors and a nurse whom he had come to know and respect. He felt frazzled from the drive and had a quick meal in a nearby truck stop before heading back to his room. He hoped that a good night's sleep would help him reclaim his energy.

As he opened the door to his room, he heard a noise and realised there was a light on. Entering, he saw the voluptuous shape that had sat next to him at the dinner in Sydney. The woman's appearance deprived Brian's imagination of work, as she was sitting on his couch dressed incongruously in a black slip and polished high heels.

'What are you doing in my room?' exclaimed Brian.

'It's Phoebe, remember?'

'I remember. But how did you know I was here, and how did you get in?'

Phoebe calmly stood up and slowly walked towards Brian. 'Look, just hear me out. I've heard what you've been going through, and I want you to know that I don't go along with it. I'm living with him, but he's a bastard. We're not married, but we have a three-year-old girl who lives with my mother in America most of the time. Can I show you something to prove I'm sorry, very sorry?' She stopped a few feet from Brian and her words began tumbling out. 'Aren't you going to invite me to stay? No, why not? I'd hoped that we could spend the night together.'

Brian listened to this torrent of words in stunned silence – and found he was determined to hold onto whatever integrity he still possessed. He believed Gill would continue to trust and love him, and there was no way he was going to betray that.

He stepped back as his emotions scripted his words. 'Look Phoebe, I do like you, I find you attractive, but I am fully committed to my relationship, with Gillian. I won't destroy that. You can keep using this room tonight and I'll check into another room.'

Against his better judgement, he then gently reached out and touched her face. 'I was worried you were being used to attack me, but I don't believe that's the case.'

His next words he regretted the moment he heard them. Almost in a whisper as if not wanting to hear the stranger within.

'It seems to me that we are both attracted to each other.' He carefully weighed his next words. 'I know how the sect works, and it could be that Ralph has been manipulated and controlled by them. There may be a slight chance that he could be helped to escape from their power, and both of you could work on your relationship.'

As if reading from a script written by a ghost writer, he whispered: 'Though it would be incredibly hard work and may very well fail. But I have to say that's for the two of you to decide. It's not for me to tell you. Either way, I wish you the best, but this will have to be the last time we meet.'

Brian turned around and left the room. He had not established how Phoebe came to know where he was, nor did he totally trust that she wasn't there to hurt him, but he mostly believed her.

After getting the key to another room from the motel's reception, he went to bed. He was very wound up, and took some medication to help him sleep. And sleep he did, a very deep sleep where reality and fantasy merged and were hard to differentiate.

Brian had a vivid dream that he chose not to share with Gillian when he went home. In it, he fed off the voluptuous body of Ralph's partner, Phoebe, hearing her moans of ecstasy. At the same time he reaped the jackpot in knowing that Ralph was gasping his last breath nearby, fully aware of who Phoebe had betrayed him for.

THE END